Madam Honey

Madam Honey

Trina Beasley

B.gl bal
Publishing

ISBN: 9780988786615

First Printing January 2014
Printed in the United States of America

Dedication

To My Parents
Yvonne Johnson and Jerry Beasley

1

Mary Ann Tobert

Mary stood at the steps of the porch as nervous as a convict standing before an electric chair. She tried to form a thought in her mind as to why she should walk away from the enormous, white, two-story house that sat a ways back, nestled in the thick forest. The dwelling seemed to be hidden and everything about it was abnormal. For one thing, the house looked too nice to be tucked way off in the woods. Its appearance gave off a humble feeling, the same feeling Mary used to get when she stepped in her grandmother's yard. It even had a large, screened wraparound porch like the one her grandmother had. Located behind the house was a big shed but, upon closer inspection, it looked too well kept to be used just for a storage place. To Mary, the shed actually appeared to be a mini-house. Glancing back at the main house before her, she noticed it was neat and orderly. Painted sparkling pearl white with light pink trimming, it held a strange innocence.

Looking around, Mary found it strange that amidst the uneven rocky soil and tall trees, there was a nice plush lawn, with all types of flowers encircling the home. Without a doubt, she knew the soil had been brought in specifically for that purpose. Flowers of such beauty as these did not grow anywhere else in the forest and only appeared on the grounds of the peculiar dwelling. Everything about the house said family; everything except the bright red light that burned through the large front picture window.

"Damn you, Travis Newton!" Mary exclaimed.

Tears welled in her eyes just thinking about the truths he had turned into lies once he had gotten her away from her momma and daddy.

Taking a deep breath, she told herself, '*This house will only be temporary. Me walking up the steps and knocking on the door will only be a phase — a phase of my life I will forget about once the ordeal is over. The moment I earn enough money, I will be able to make good on life. Then I will be able to return home with more than a broken heart to show for my time away.*'

"They smell weakness around these parts and the smell of fear makes 'em attack."

Startled by the stranger's voice, Mary turned toward the direction it had come from and spotted a short, red-headed, pretty woman standing behind her. Mary's first thought was that the woman looked different. Though she was attractive — about five-one, thick, but not fat, and sported a bright smile with a set of perfect white teeth —what made her look a bit odd was her build. At first glance, the lady looked like a white woman but her body was more like a black one—full hips and a big, round butt. The last thing Mary had expected to see was a white woman in a black woman's whorehouse.

"You wanna make sure you good and ready before you walk through that there door," the stranger said, pointing toward the entrance of the house as she spoke.

"Ain't no love once you step across that threshold. People making plenty of love with they bodies, but ain't no love in nobody's heart around these here parts. On second thought, it ain't love we making. We simply be screwing." The woman spat on the ground before continuing. "But at least we can take pride and say we get paid for our services. They ain't respectable services, but they are services that are well needed. If not, we wouldn't be in such high demand."

Mary stood calmly, trying to digest the information that had been given to her by this bold stranger. "You Madam Honey?" she finally asked, breaking the silence.

"Naw, chile." the redhead said, letting out a hearty laugh. "They call me Cherry on account that I'm damn near white. Hell, if I ever have a baby by a white man, my chile wouldn't be considered black at all. I know I look full peckerwood. That's 'cause my momma was almost white. My daddy, they tell me, was a high-yella nigga. Then, there is some that say he was a full-blooded white man. Me, myself, I don't care too much what he was 'cause he ain't never did a damn thing for me. Truth be told, I did more for him. It was 'cause of me he was able to get a piece of pleasure the night I was created. Don't look at me that way. I'm known for telling the truth. I simply tell things the way they are.

"Being almost white didn't help my momma none 'cause she was treated like a full-blooded nigga. Me looking white ain't helped me none, either. All these folks around here know my momma was part nigga. I learned long ago not to waste my thoughts on 'could-of-should-of-would-of.' I am what I am. Ain't no use in wishing I was something else. Folks around here refer to me as the white nigga whore. I been around these parts all my life. My momma got tired of her white nigga baby bringing her life to a stop. Story is, she met a fine white man and went off to Europe pretending that I didn't exist. I hear they don't look down on white men for loving black women in Europe. At least that's what I heard. She did grant me enough courtesy to drop me off at Madam Honey's before she left, though. I look at it this way: she could have dropped me off on the side of a dirt road and went on 'bout her life. I ain't mad at her no more. If I was her, I probably would have done the same thing.

"Besides, if I was full white, these folks around here would hang Madam Honey's big ass from one of these tall trees. In this day and time, people don't take kindly to white women sleeping with black men, at least not here in Florida. They don't mind white men buying pussy from black women, but you turn things the other way around and shit is bound to burn. These peckerwoods would burn this whole town down, but not before hanging plenty strange fruit on all those trees in the forest. I hear some white lady a town over started sleeping with her yard boy. Fool went so far as to have a baby by him. My thinking is she must have thought the baby was gonna turn out like me —looking all white. Anyways, the baby didn't. They tell me the baby girl she had was a beauty, but that didn't do the chile no good. Soon as the doctor laid eyes on her, he pulled the umbilical cord off the infant and let it bleed to death. The colored fool who got her momma pregnant left town before anything could happen to him. Soon after, the white woman died of some mysterious ailment that suddenly came about. No, the south dictates who will be sleeping with who."

Mary did not know how to respond to Cherry's remarks. The one thing she did understand about this stranger was that she was used to hard living. Mary sensed that Cherry was not the type to feel sorry for herself —or anybody else for that matter. She seemed like the type who was working with the hand she was dealt. No, it was not a proper hand, but Mary had to admit, Cherry was playing it to the best of her ability.

"Walk into town with me and have a drink," Cherry said, taking Mary by the hand.

"I don't drink," Mary managed to say.

"What?!"Cherry said with a look of disbelief on her face. "Well, if you plan on moving into Madam Honey's house, you better start drinking. I might as well be the one who introduces you to the liquid sinfulness that's gonna aid in saving your sanity. You don't wanna recall half the stuff you did with strange men come morning. You best learn to start saying you used to not drink, 'cause you gonna need plenty drinks in order to take up residence in the house I live in."

Cherry grabbed Mary's arm and led her through the forest.

"They got plenty to eat and drink in Madam Honey's house. It's good food, too. I just go to town to get away. You stay around there too long and everything that's going on in that house becomes normal. I got enough sense left in my head to know how I'm living is wicked. I figure I got to live to the best of my ability. My best ability is pleasing men. It ain't my fault most all the men I please belong to somebody else. I didn't go looking for them. They came and requested me. Not to toot my own horn, but I'm *damn* good at pleasing," she said with a smirk.

"I tries to get away from the house as much as I can. I'm an outcast there. The loner." Cherry let out a carefree laugh. "They don't too much care for me. It figures. My momma didn't so I don't take how they treat me personal."

2

Madam Honey (Abigail Richard)

Madam Honey walked into the living room and sat down on the loveseat. She wore a white housecoat and a pair of white house shoes.

'Gonna be real busy tonight,' thought with a look of pleasure in her small beady eyes.

"Y'all needs to get y'all selves together." Madam Honey turned to Toni and said, "Tonight the girls have to be extra-nice looking. Tonight ain't like any other night. Tonight is special. The Mayor is having his victory celebration. I'm sho' glad he won. If he was ever to lose, things wouldn't be the same for us. Lord knows I owe the Mayor plenty of thanks. I thank God every day that He allow me to run my establishment the way I see fit with no disruption.

"He's been allowing it since he been in office. When he wasn't, his daddy let me run the place without having to worry about the law breaking down my door and hauling all my girls off to jail. I can remember when the Mayor's daddy brought him in to get his first piece of tail..." Madam Honey let out a strong laugh. "Yeah, the Mayor and me go way back. That's why things have to be perfect tonight.

"He sho' enjoys the appreciation the girls show him 'specially since his wife has been having them bed problems. I hear she still mourning the death of their son. The boy's been dead nearly five years. Imagine that! She hasn't slept with him in five whole years. I cain't imagine not sleeping with my own husband for five years. That woman needs some special kind of counseling. Money won't be flowing tonight, but that's all right this one time— but only this time."

Madam Honey took time to catch her breath before continuing.

"Where the hell is Cherry? She knows she's the Mayor's number one request— well, her and Chocolate. That man sho' is a freak. He enjoys his white meat as well as dark." She picked up the jar on the end table and pulled out a pickled pig ear with her large hands.

Toni replied, "I seen her walking towards town with some tall, brown, shapely woman. The woman must be new to these parts 'cause I ain't never seen her around here before. You know how Cherry is. She likes to go into town every now and again. Why? I don't know. She jumps up and heads out of here like she got somebody waiting for her. The way she leaves you'd think she had an appointment or something. She knows as well as everybody in town that ain't nobody in high spirits when she arrives. Ain't a soul in town who wants to be bothered with her silly white ass. Anybody that wants to see her comes here after respectable visiting hours."

"In town?" Madam Honey said with a hint of anger in her voice. She dropped the half-eaten pig ear on the floor. "What would make her do something so damn crazy? It's too late to be dragging around town drinking and carrying on. She has work to do around here. I cain't stand for her to be acting like she don't have a job to do. She know better than any of y'all how important tonight is. She been doing this since she was a little girl. Things have always been the way they are today. The Mayor and his friends have always been given a day of appreciation. She knows today of all days ain't the day for her to wandering off and going to town. Get my garlic cloves. That girl done made my pressure rise."

"You know Cherry ain't never been much on thinking," Toni commented as she picked the pig ear up from the floor and walked through the swinging doors into the kitchen.

"Well," Madam Honey yelled in Toni's direction as she readjusted her six-foot, three hundred and thirty-something pound frame on the loveseat, "as long as she keeps bringing me plenty greenbacks, I'm not gonna worry about her brains! As long as her bottom stays busy we won't have no problems. Besides, regardless of what you think about her, Cherry do a whole lot better than yo' girl Chocolate. She may be a little silly when it comes to thinking standing on her feet, but she got plenty brains when it comes to lying on her back."

Hearing Madam Honey's pronouncement, Toni rolled her eyes, turned and walked back into the kitchen where she quietly stood for a moment gazing out the window. No matter how irritated she got with Madam Honey, Toni knew the worst thing in the world she could do was to make the massive woman angry.

Actually, Toni would have done better by simply leaving the house and finding somewhere else to stay. It was rumored Madam Honey had killed twenty people—fifteen whores and five johns. Toni did not know how true the number was but she had personally witnessed Madam Honey take out two johns and one whore. The johns had disrespected her and the whore, Sunshine, had held out on her. Sunshine was not only stealing from the johns, she was stealing from Madam Honey, as well.

Sheriff Jenkins had simply come in, cleaned up the murders and made them look as if they had all been in self-defense. It was generally understood that as long as Madam Honey did not kill a white man, she was in the clear. White problems were handled directly by Sheriff Jenkins. Madam Honey would send for him as soon as she smelled trouble and he would be there in a heartbeat. Everybody in town —white or black — knew she paid top-dollar for her personal protection.

"How the girl look; the one she left with?" Madam Honey asked when Toni re-entered the living room.

As Toni handed Madam Honey the garlic cloves, she replied, "She was tall, real tall. 'Bout as tall as you. Somebody must have sent her this way 'cause I cain't see her stumbling on this place by accident."

"Must be looking for work," Madam Honey said with a greedy grin on her face. She stopped talking and swallowed three cloves whole. "I sho' hope so 'cause, since Violet left, my intake hasn't been the same and no matter my intake, Sheriff Jenkins wants his cut. Was she good-looking?" The look on her face revealed that she was hungry for the money the stranger could possibly soon bring in for her.

Before answering, Toni glanced around. She wanted to make sure Chocolate was not within hearing distance.

Lowering her voice, she answered, "Yes, Lord!" Her eyes lit up when she spoke. "A six-foot beauty. She had a delicate mahogany complexion and a head full of soft wavy hair. Her ponytail hung down to the middle of her back."

"What she built like?" Madam Honey asked.

"She was shaped like an hour-glass. She looked to be a money-maker to me," Toni stated.

"Good. I got me a white one, a black one, a yellow one, and now I'll have me a brown one. Variety is always good for business. Get me a cold drink of tea, please."

Toni rushed to the kitchen and hurriedly brought back a glass of tea.

As she eagerly handed the tea to Madam Honey, the older woman told her, "You might as well wipe that silly wanting grin off your face. Chocolate will kill both of y'all if she catches you snooping in behind that girl. Besides, you don't even know if she's into women."

"Chocolate wasn't into women until I got a hold of her."

"Well, regardless of what Chocolate told you, you might as well get this new girl off your mind. Ain't gonna be no blood shedding around here lessen I'm the one pulling the trigger. You got that?"

After making her pronouncement, Madam Honey struggled to get her obese body up and out of the loveseat. Once up, she headed out to the wraparound porch where she intended to sit in her favorite rocker. Maybe she would spot Cherry and the newcomer coming back from town, enabling her to assess her future earnings.

3

Mary Ann Tobert

Y ou want kids?" Mary finally asked, breaking the silence at the table.

Cherry had taken Mary to the only all-black drinking establishment in town. The bar, unlike Madam Honey's home, was owned and ran by a white man. It was a small place, run down and dirty. There were only five tables inside the bar and the door was barely hanging on its hinges. Mary looked in amazement at the flow of drunken men and women stumbling in and out. Wrinkling her nose in distaste, she detected the combined strong smell of piss, vomit and powerful body odor.

Mary did not intend to get personal with the white/black stranger who sat across the dirty table from her. The fact was her own baby, the one who died, stayed on her mind. She did not know what pained her the most—losing the baby or losing Travis. Originally, Mary had reasoned that the baby would tie Travis down— make him stay put. Her only hope had been that they try again. Instead, after the baby died, he left.

Cherry thought a moment then answered, "Ain't never thought that far in the future. I think I pretty much stopped dreaming when I landed at Madam Honey's house. I don't even recall any of my dreams before coming to Madam Honey's. I'm pretty sure I did have a dream, on account that all girls dream of being something one day. I can tell you this, though, I ain't never thought I'd end up selling my ass to make ends meet. I been doing it so long, I cain't imagine a feeling coming with the process. I cain't imagine loving a man after he gets off of me. When I was younger, I used to get caught up in all that shit."

As if remembering something pleasant, a light smile spread across Cherry's face before she continued, "Believe me when I say I done had some good ones lay on top of me. I done had more than my share of good sessions. But the older I got, I began to realize that's all they were. They were good, but they all belonged to somebody else. I learned to leave that type of thinking alone—the type of thinking that has to do with love. A long time ago, that type of thinking died."

Momentarily looking at Mary, Cherry noticed the strange look on the girl's face.

"Nowadays, I just stack my money. I focus on what it is his money is gonna buy me after he gets off of me. This is the way I see things now. No matter how good he makes me feel, no matter how nice he talks to me, when he pulls out, I remind myself he already got somebody that he love enough to take home to his momma. He might tell his friend, brother, even his daddy about but his momma won't know about me until Judgement Day and he won't be the one telling.

"No, Mary, I don't dream anymore. I figure I'll buy whatever dream I decide to have in the future. I know you cain't buy children, but I don't plan on children being part of my future wants. Besides, every time somebody gets pregnant at Madam Honey's, she mixes up this strange sour-tasting concoction. You drink it and the baby is a memory. I've drank it a few times. I figure if I ever get pregnant and wanted the chile, I won't have her make me the baby-killing poison.

Babies and prostitution don't mix. A baby would get in the way of my moneymaking skills. Instead of saving money I'd be spending it on the little bastard. Plus, a man would lose his mind if he thought a whore was carrying his chile. I'm willing to bet he'd kill you."

Mary's eyes enlarged upon hearing Cherry's comment about the baby-killing poison.

Seeing her reaction, Cherry said, "Girl, it ain't as bad as you think. It's not like you killing a real baby. The baby ain't the size of an apple. I've seen what it looks like with my own eyes. It's just a little ball of blood. Ain't no arms or legs attached to it. The thing ain't even got a head or a body, just blood. Madam Honey will only give it to you if you are two or three weeks late. You come crying to her when you are a month or two late and she'll put you out of her house."

Cherry took a swig of her drink and made a hard face. "Once, she gave this girl the drink when she was two months with chile. She must have been carrying the baby in her hips and back 'cause couldn't nobody tell she was that far along. Poor girl bled to death. She laid on the floor crying and screaming for God or anybody else who was near her. Madam Honey called for the doctor, but there was nothing that could be done. He couldn't stop the bleeding. It was an awful death. Before she died, she had a nice even brown complexion. I saw her body when the screaming was done. She had turned deep purple, almost black. I think all the blood had drained from her body. Poor girl screamed herself into a different skin tone.

"The girl drank the mixture around eight that morning. The process should have taken two or three hours. Instead of the usual time, it took all day and most of the night. The poor child's suffering wasn't over until around two that morning. Men came and were turned away. There was no way Madam Honey could conduct business with all that mess taking place in her establishment. She probably would have opened up if it wasn't for the blood. The smell of it was so strong it took Toni three bottles of ammonia and a box of baking soda to get the foul odor out of the house. And to be honest, it still was there weeks after the girl's death.

"Personally, I think Madam Honey was pissed off 'cause she had to shut down for a night. You ain't heard this from me, but Madam Honey is the meanest woman you ever gonna lay eyes on. She is what you call 'money crazy.' Her only concern is money. If you slack off or try and steal from her, she'll put you six feet under quicker than you can blink. Now, I'm only speaking on what I know, not what I've heard."

After listening to Cherry, Mary picked up her glass of bourbon. Earlier she'd told herself that she was not going to touch the glass of brown liquor the waiter had placed in front of her. She had actually pleaded with Cherry to purchase her an orange soda. But Cherry had ignored the plea and instructed the waiter to bring two tall glasses of bourbon and ice.

Now, cautiously, Mary tasted the drink. It tasted bad —real bad. But after hearing what she was about to get herself into, Mary ignored the taste. She noticed that even though the liquid was cold, it burned her insides as it slid down her throat and all the way into her stomach.

Looking at the face Mary had made upon tasting the liquor, Cherry let out her now famous laugh and said, "Taste ain't so good, but it will help you deal with the new life you are about to embark on. Look at it like this," she said in a somber tone, "if you looking to make some money, Madam Honey's the right place. You young, you pretty. Baby girl, you got potential. But once you stroll through her doors, there is no turning back. If it's money you want to get, get it and keep moving. Mary, if you looking for a good time, you'll get more than your share of that, also. Just know that once you enter my world, the outside world won't accept you no more, at least not around here.

"I'm not trying to keep you or run you off. I'm simply giving you what most folks won't offer—the God's honest truth. I could sit here and tell you a bunch of lies. We both know lies is easy. I could tell you that you in for the time of your life. I could focus on the men and all the good things they will say and all the money they will pay. I'd earn a few brownie points with Madam Honey if I did. You ain't the kind that I'm used to seeing walk through her door. You ain't a whore. But I know you can readily be turned into one. I know that just 'cause you ain't one now don't mean you won't turn into one tomorrow. You looks more like the housewife type—the type that used to despise me; not the type who want to be me."

Mary could feel the liquor loosening her up. She wondered why this white/black woman was looking after her best interests. True, Mary heard the statement about why she said she was giving her this bit of information, but Mary was not so sure she should believe it.

As Mary listened to Cherry rumble on about life, her mind wondered back into time, thinking, *'If only Travis wouldn't have left.'*

She knew what she wanted and it was not this information Cherry was telling her concerning life as a whore. She did not want to know the 'dos and don'ts of sleeping with strange men. What she wanted was to go home; back to Wichita, Kansas, the small town she once had hated, but now needed.

'What I wouldn't give right now to stroll through a field of sunflowers or sit on the edge of a muddy lake and swing my feet

through the murky water, or, better yet, a game of hide-and-seek in a cornfield would satisfy me at this very moment,' she thought.

Thinking about her grandmother's homemade ice cream made from fresh Kansas snow caused Mary to take a big swallow of air. She even found herself craving the tornadoes that sometimes terrorized her hometown and tore some parts of the city to shreds. Even the snowstorms that trapped everybody in their homes for days-on- end did not seem so bad, anymore.

Mary knew that going home was out of the question. The day she sided with Travis against her was the day her old life ended. Even though Mary's mind told her he was wrong, her heart told her differently. After all, he had promised Mary that if she left and went with him, he would make her his wife. Instead, he had taken her all the way to Florida just to abandon her. He had not even bothered to tell her goodbye. Brokenhearted, she figured his itch had acted up. That itch of his had to be the only reason he had left her. On a Sunday he had been acting strange. He left on Monday.

No, home was not a place where she could return. Naturally, Mary had tried calling. She honestly had thought that once she informed her mother of her situation, all would be forgiven. Her mother had listened, said nothing, then hung up the phone. Worried and upset, Mary had waited a few days and tried calling back. The number had been changed. Mary reasoned her mother had sided with her father, just as she had sided with Travis.

Coming back to the present, Mary finally blurted out to Cherry, "I need some money."

"You don't seem like the wicked type. Have you tried honest work?" Cherry asked.

"I'm not trained in anything that will pay me enough to live on my own."

"Well, I tell you one thing; once you settle in at Madam Honey's, ain't nobody in this town gonna give you a chance to find a job that will permit you to live on your own. Truth be told, they'd lock me out of town if they could."

Cherry picked up the glass and finished off her liquor before she continued, "See that old man over there?" She pointed to the man standing over the grill. "He likes grapes and nuts strung about his entire asshole. I'd be willing to bet my entire month's salary his wife has no idea. They been married twenty-something years and she still don't know the man."

"How you know?" Mary asked in astonishment.

"He's been one of my regulars since I entered Madam Honey's establishment. He's been visiting me two times a month, every other Tuesday, like clockwork. You get to know people when you sleep with 'em for a living. Me stepping outside of those woods makes these townsmen a little nervous. Though they ignore me during daylight hours, they love me when the sun goes down."

"I don't plan on making this my home. I just need a way to make a quick buck," Mary said, sounding as if she was trying to convince herself and not Cherry.

"Well, making a quick buck is what Madam Honey is all about." Cherry stood up from the table indicating that she was ready to leave. "I think it's best we head on over and I introduce you to the heavy, pistol-packing queen of the forest. She's not as bad as people make her out to be. You work hard and she'll pay you good.

Whatever you do, don't try and steal from her. I done seen many a whore meet her maker behind trying to mess with Madam Honey's money. She'll shoot you over fifty-cents. Madam Honey always says, 'If you steal from me, then you'll kill me.' I guess she intend to kill the thief first."

Mary finished off her drink and wobbled out of the chair. Being drunk was a new experience for her. It was not as bad as she had thought it would be. In fact, life seemed less painful with the warm alcohol flowing through her veins. For the first time in a long time, she was not even feeling sorry for herself. For the first time in a long time, she was able to put thoughts of her baby's death aside— the baby Travis did not seem to give a damn about because, had he cared, he would have never left her alone. She was now forced to live with the awful memory by herself.

She thought, '*What I wouldn't give to see Travis at this very moment. Instead of begging him to take me back, I would cuss the life out of him. Not only would I cuss him, I would slap him down the way he done my father.*

"She's gonna rename you," Cherry said, interrupting Mary's thoughts as they walked through the forest. "She does that to everybody. My real name is Heather. Heather Lee Witman. I had me a dignified sounding name, but it didn't fit my personality. I think I act more like a Cherry. Heather is a decent, Christian-sounding name. I ain't decent and never have been. Madam Honey took one look at me and said my new name was Cherry on account that I was a white/black girl with cherry-red hair. She said men would love the feel of cherries in their mouths and between their legs. I ain't been called Heather in so long, I have to remind myself it's my real name."

4

Madam Honey (Abigail Richard)

W here the hell you been?" Madam Honey barked as soon as Cherry and Mary stepped through the big front door.

The easy warm feeling that calmed Mary's nerves and made her forget about her problems disappeared as soon as she laid eyes on the gigantic, abnormal-looking woman.

'*She got to be at least half a foot taller than me,*' Mary thought. She had never seen a person like Madam Honey in her life.

"Cherry," Madam Honey roared, "you get on upstairs and get yo' self ready for the Mayor! Chocolate been waitin' on you all day! You gonna get enough of runnin' off to town. You know better than to leave out of here on such an important day."

Cherry headed up the stairs without a word.

"What we got here?" Madam Honey said eyeing Mary like she was the last piece of candy on the shelf. Madam Honey's mood went from angry to gentle and kind in a matter of seconds. The loud and raspy voice Mary had heard just seconds before had suddenly turned soft and tender. "Somethin' in my big bones tells me you lookin' for employment. Looks to me like you pretty green, but that ain't a problem. We was all virgins at one point in our lives. It's been so long for me I done forgot how being one feels. I tell you one thing: if you a quick learner and hard worker, you done came to the right place. Come on around here and have a seat."

Mary momentarily caught her foot on a loose pull in the thick velvet carpet. She almost stumbled once more when she noticed the large indentations Madam Honey's weight left in the carpet. Silently, Mary swallowed hard as she witnessed the woman's large frame cover both cushions on the gigantic scarlet couch as she sat down.

'She's got to be the oddest looking woman God ever created,' Mary thought as she observed the huge woman trying to maneuver into a comfortable position. At the same time, she realized that Madam Honey's breathing was the loudest she had ever heard coming from a human being who was not running. There was some natural consternation in her mind, as Mary was not quite sure how to take the huge creature sitting across from her.

In fascination, Mary continued to observe this puzzling and unusual looking person. Madam Honey wore a thick, nappy, blond wig on her head that did not look good against her tree-bark brown complexion. Not only was she the color of a tree, but her skin was as rough as one. Mary could not figure out if the wig was too small or if it was pulled back on her head too far. Due to the fact that the wig was not on properly, the graying edges of her own hair stuck out here and there, adding to her weird look. It was not simply her hair and size that made her look so creepy, there were deep dark circles around her small, beady, dark brown eyes. Also, she had dark, silver dollar-sized spots all over her arms and ankles. Mary could not help but wonder if the spots covered her entire body.

"Cherry tell you how I run things around here?" Madam Honey asked.

"A little bit," Mary said softly.

"Speak up, chile. Don't be whisperin' when you talkin' to me. You save that soft baby voice for the men. They like all that nonsense. Me? I like to hear what a person has to say to me."

"Some," Mary said louder.

"Well, here's my rules: I get seventy-five percent of what you make. May sound high, but you don't ever have to worry about the law haulin' you in. Sheriff Jenkins is one of our best customers. The Mayor will drop by sometimes, also. The deal is, I send the men in, you please 'em. You want a drink?"

"Yes," Mary said, feeling she needed another one.

"What you drinkin'?"

"Bourbon," Mary gave the answer like it was not the second time in her life she had ever consumed alcohol.

"Toni!" Madam Honey yelled.

Just when Mary thought she had seen it all, a female, who resembled a man, walked into the living room. Toni— as Madam Honey had called her— wore black slacks, a men's dress shirt, and two-toned black and white Stacey Adams. Her head was shaved bald and she had a thin line of eyeliner penciled in over her top lip. Mary could not help but stare and at the same time wonder, *'Where on earth did this small-framed man-woman come from?'*

It was obvious that, although Toni gave the appearance of a man, anyone who laid eyes on her knew that Toni could be a beautiful woman if she desired.

"Get us something to drink…two glasses of bourbon," Toni hurried out of the room and shortly returned with the drinks. Mary watched in amazement as Madam Honey swallowed her drink in one noisy gulp.

"This yo' first time workin' on yo' back?" Madam Honey abruptly asked.

"Yes," Mary whispered. The look on Madam Honey's face notified her that she was speaking too low. "I don't plan on doing it for long," Mary said louder. "I'm in a bind. I figure it cain't be too hard to learn. I came here with a man, but it didn't work out. I figure I gotta do something 'cause I refuse to return home empty-handed."

"Well, you can stay as long as you follow my rules. Tryin' to steal is the one thing that will get you hurt around here. It's gotten a few killed. I know what's due to me at the end of the night and I expect it. I'm not one for excuses 'bout why you short. I'll start you off slow. I won't send no real freaks to your room, but just know they comin'. Where's yo' clothes and such?"

"I left everything at the room I was renting. I'll have to wait before I can get my things. I don't have the money to pay for the time I spent there. I didn't know if you'd accept me. The woman who told me about you said I should first come and talk to you."

"We'll get you some things to put on. I'll have Toni show you to your room. Toni!" Madam Honey yelled again. Just like that, Toni appeared out of nowhere. "Take this gal up to the empty room. She's gonna be stayin' with us."

Mary stood and turned to follow Toni.

"Bit-of-Honey."

Hearing this, Mary turned and faced Madam Honey looking confused.

"That's what your new name is. You look like a taste of something golden brown and sweet."

5

Toni (Rainie Holloway)

Toni ran the razor across her scalp once more before placing it on the table next to the bed she shared with Chocolate. The night had gone smoothly and she was glad it was over. Madam Honey had not allowed any paying customers in the house. All of the girls were strictly for the Mayor and his crew. Good thing Bit-of-Honey showed up when she did because Cherry, Chocolate and Pretty would have had to put in overtime.

Toni giggled to herself when she thought how impatiently the Mayor's men had waited to take their turns with the women. The three who looked most absurd had been Big Bubba, Skinny Len and Charles. Big Bubba had seemed to sweat a puddle of nerves. Skinny Len was apple-red in the face and Charles kept rubbing his groin and humming. Sheriff Jenkins always came alone.

This was the only time when these men came to Madam Honey's. They were what the town referred to as "respectable men." Two were deacons of the church and the other was the treasurer. They could not be seen with the common men who frequented Madam Honey's establishment because they were well-known town leaders.

"She did all right for somebody who's supposedly new at this," Chocolate announced to Toni as she entered the bedroom.

"Who?" Toni asked, pretending not to know who Chocolate was referring to. Toni felt Chocolate was testing her. Lately, Chocolate seemed to be looking for any reason to be upset with her.

"That Little Honey, Bit-of-Honey, or whatever the hell Madam Honey calls her. She's gonna have to learn how to handle her liquor, 'cause I do believe that girl was drunk as Cootie Brown by the time the second man entered her room. Ain't no telling what Charles had her doin'. That Charles is a slick one. I'm more than sure he got a little extra out of her.

"Damn, I'm tired," she said taking off her wig. "That vinegar and baking soda bath seems to have put me closer to sleep. I guess I soaked in the tub too long."

"You worked pretty hard tonight. I'm pretty sure Big Bubba put in overtime, too," commented Toni, slyly looking Chocolate's way.

"Please," Chocolate said rolling her eyes. "Big Bubba liked to got his rocks off before my robe hit the ground. Bubba all talk and no action. I tell you one thing. He sho' know how to sweat. Whenever that man is on top of me, I feel like I'm in a lake or somethin'. He makes me feel like I'm drownin' in my own bed. I'm 'bout tired of Big Bubba and the rest of these sorry-ass fools that frequent this place. Here lately, I been carrying this feeling in my bones that there is more to life than the way I'm living it."

Chocolate got quiet for a moment, then said, "Maybe I want to be called Judy instead of Chocolate. Nobody around here got a decent name. We all named to resemble some pleasure feeling or object. I ain't no damn Chocolate and Pretty ain't all that damn pretty."

Sliding off her robe, Chocolate's naked body was revealed briefly before she wrapped up in a separate set of sheets and lay on the bed. "Maybe I'm done with this phase of my life. My father's cousin did always say I was a confused chile. Said I was never quite sure of what it was I intended to get out of life. I done did a whole lot of living and I'm just now considering her being right. I cain't too much blame myself for not listening to her. She wasn't what you would call nice to me. Matter of fact, she mistreated me my entire life."

Toni was not sure how to respond to Chocolate's comment. The subjects mentioned did not fit into their relationship. Never before had she spoken about her upbringing. She used to speak about how happy Toni made her feel, how Toni was her new independence, her new expression. In return for the new feeling, Toni assumed she was providing all the love Chocolate needed. Now she was coming to realize that she did not really know Chocolate.

Toni had noticed awhile back that Chocolate was changing. For one thing, she did not spend money like she used to. It puzzled Toni that she was saving. There had been a time when Chocolate would buy everything she set her eyes on. Packages never stopped arriving at the house addressed to her. As a matter of a fact, that's how Toni had found out her real name, Judy Brown. She had ordered anything from fancy dresses, golden bracelets, to expensive candies.

Madam Honey was always complaining about the way Chocolate spent her money. "You need to put something up for a rainy day. You ain't always gonna be able to charge such high prices for your bottom. All those fancy clothes ain't gonna be able to fit you when you old and gravity pulls everything south. You gonna look at those high-dollar clothes for their worth—not a damn thing.

Time flies and you gonna look up one day and wonder why the hell you wasted all your money."

In response, Chocolate would let out a little giggle and open her packages.

About six months before, all the useless spending had stopped. Instead of buying anything she wanted, Chocolate took to looking for deals. Nowadays, she was venturing over to the used clothing stores to buy her clothes. She even took to wearing fake, discolored jewelry. One of her johns, Mr. Peter, must have noticed because he bought her a set of diamond earrings. Chocolate took the earrings and sold them. What she did with the money was a mystery to Toni.

The change Toni hated most was what was taking place in their bedroom. It had taken her— what felt like a lifetime— to find a woman who respected how she felt about women. Before Chocolate, all her encounters with women were secret and they were either drunk or wanted to experiment. Chocolate was different. She allowed Toni to come to her bed not because she wanted to try something new, but because she wanted to be with somebody who was interested in more than just sex. Chocolate had made it clear that she was not interested in women.

Slowly, Toni had built a friendship with Chocolate. After awhile, a special bond had formed between the two women. Chocolate explained that she had never had a female friend before. On account of her being a whore, women tended to stay clear of her. "But, I like you. I think I like you the way you like me," she'd told Toni. With those words, a "loveship" was formed. Toni finally had her first non-secret lover.

Chocolate did not mind the girls turning their noses up at her for holding Toni's hand or sitting on her lap during the daylight hours. It was Toni who felt uncomfortable. She was not used to having somebody openly care for her the way she had always dreamed. After awhile, she stopped being ashamed of Chocolate and accepted her.

But recently, things had changed. Toni did not know how to handle Chocolate's rejection. She had no idea where it was coming from. First, she thought Chocolate had fallen in love with a man. She knew because it happened all the time. That was the reason Violet had up and run off a few months back. She did not as much as tell Madam Honey bye or kiss her ass. She simply left to go shopping and never returned. In fact, she had not even taken a suitcase. Later, word got back to Madam Honey that Violet had high-tailed it out of town with Phil.

Phil was ten years younger than Violet. She had taken his virginity and he had lost his mind. Madam Honey tried introducing him to one of the other girls, but Phil refused. All he wanted was Violet; either he would have her or he refused to spend. All the girls saw it coming. It got to the point that, when he paid to see her, they fussed the whole time. Through the walls, Toni heard him crying about her having to be with other men.

Upon examining Chocolate's case, Toni realized it was not a Phil situation. Chocolate had no new lovers coming around. She was not spending any extra time with any of her old johns. Chocolate was battling a different type of demon.

Tired was always the excuse for her not wanting to be intimate with Toni, which did not add up because there was a time when no matter how many johns she saw, she was able to keep

Chocolate up until the noon hours. In fact, she could not get enough of Toni. Here lately, she wrapped herself up in her own set of covers and went to sleep right away. It was not any pretend sleep, either. It seemed as soon as Chocolate closed her eyes, a deep snore set in.

Looking at her sleeping, Toni wanted to shake Chocolate and wake her up. There were questions she needed answered, but feared asking them. She did not think she could return to the world of sneaking around with women. What she needed was Chocolate. Chocolate made love easy, made loving women easy. Without her, Toni would be a lone outcast forced to take the small handouts of affection which she had once lived off of.

She pushed her separate covered body as close as she could to Chocolate's and whispered to her sleeping lover, "We'll talk. Whatever it is, I'll help make it right."

6

Mary Ann Tobert (Bit-of-Honey)

W asn't as bad as you thought it would be," Cherry announced, opening the door and stepping into Mary's room. The room was just as the other the girls' — dark paint on the walls, a large bed in the middle of the floor, a full-length mirror and a solid wood dresser. A white porcelain wash bowl was pushed in the corner and a white dingy washrag was on the floor next to it. It was the first time Mary had seen Cherry sober and without makeup. She looked like a tired old woman.

"You'll be the number one attraction around here for awhile. The new girls always get plenty action. I'm gonna tell you something I ain't never let out of the bag."

"What?" Mary sat up on the bed.

"If you wanna keep them coming, you gotta come up with a trick. My specialty is giving pleasure with my mouth. Most of these girls don't like doing it. If you don't like doing something, then you don't do it well. I don't expect you to be a pro with it in a day. But when you do it, pretend it's the best thing in the world. Make 'em feel like they yo' favorite flavor. That goes for whatever takes place in the bed. I don't care how gross you feel about the lame-ass sucker, you gotta make him think you not only like him, but that you love him. Give the impression that you would do him for free. You do that and he'll tip you. He'll tip you good. The money Madam Honey gives you won't compare to what he'll give you. So, what did you think about last night?"

"I don't recall much." Then Mary's face screwed up in a terrible frown and she yelled, "Ugh! I ain't never smelled this bad in my entire life!"

"You need to soak in some red vinegar and baking soda. The smell will come right off. Men always running around talking about how bad whores smell. What most people don't understand is that we don't smell bad until the men crawl off of us," Cherry explained, trying to be helpful.

"You got that right," Mary said, still frowning from the heavy, fishy, musty smell that permeated the room.

"You got plenty of time to soak 'cause the party don't start until after dinner. Madam Honey don't allow men to stop by until we been fed and rested up. To average folk it sounds like she gives a damn but, the truth is, she don't want no excuses as to why we cain't perform. Vinegar is in the closet and the baking soda is right next to it. You might want to wash before you come down. Madam Honey get a whiff of you and she's bound to pull her gun. I'll see you downstairs." With that parting advice, Cherry walked out of the room.

Mary sat in a chair next to the bed, somewhat in a daze, her mind tried to digest all that had happened to her in the past twenty-four hours. Within that short time frame, she had met a white/black girl, had her first taste of liquor, and sold her body.

'*It wasn't that bad. Actually, most of the night was a blur. After that third drink, I don't recall much of what happened. I do remember the sight of Madam Honey's large, vulgar frame standing at the door and introducing me as the "new main attraction" and a skinny, white, young-looking boy standing at my door. That was about all I can remember concerning the night. I'm not sure, but I seem to vaguely recall taking at least three other men into my bed. Probably best I stay drunk while I work this gig,'* she thought.

She stood and gathered the shirt and cutoff pants that Toni had given her. Walking to the closet, Mary found the red vinegar and a large box of baking soda.

"Boy, do I need this," she muttered to herself. Stepping out of her room, she heard the water running in the bathroom that was located in the room next to hers. She turned and walked to the bathroom at the other end of the hall. Three bathrooms were a lifesaver for a whorehouse.

Cherry had informed Mary, "This house used to belong to some crazy white woman whose husband died and left her the house. She then took up with a young, trashy-type white fella. Rumor was that he poisoned the woman and her spirit drove him crazy. Since most of the townspeople believed it, they stayed away from the house. Madam Honey, on the other hand, said she wasn't afraid of nothing dead. She took to living in the house and made it what it is today."

Upon hearing the history of the house, Mary was too worried about her own future to be taken in by it. At the moment, she was simply grateful the woman had enough sense to put in three full bathrooms—two upstairs and one downstairs.

With her eyes closed, Mary soaked in the strong mixture of red vinegar and baking soda and tried to find peace of mind. Yet, each time she closed her eyes and tried to ponder a better day, a clear picture of her father lying beaten down on the ground appeared in her head. Before that day, Mary had never seen her father in such a condition. She had never heard her father raise his voice. He was always a calm man —a man who did not believe in violence. But on that particular day, her daddy had stood up for what he loved. He fought for his only child's life.

He had lost the battle and Mary was now beginning to feel as if she had also lost her life. She needed to make things right between her and her father. She needed to make things right between her and her mother also, because, even though her daddy had taken a physical beating, it was her mother who had suffered the most. Mary knew without a doubt that if it had been her father who had answered the phone the day she called, he would have let her come home.

After thinking the situation over awhile, Mary decided not to try and get the new phone number and call again. She realized that living with her father's forgiveness under her mother's hatred was not something she could bring herself to do.

Now, she realized her mother had been correct. Many times she had told Mary, "That boy don't want you. He just playing with you. He's cut from a different piece of cloth. He cain't be tamed. You need to find you somebody who will give you a ring before he get at your panties.

"Why would he marry you, Mary? Don't look at me like I'm talking crazy. I know what y'all up to when you come home looking all silly and lovesick. I can smell the sex on you every time he drops you off at the door. I hate to be the one to inform you, but you the only one in love. You going with him. He ain't going back with you.

"What's gonna happen is, he gonna get bored with you and trade you in for a new one. Treat you like you a car or some other material object. You making it way too easy for him. His kind wouldn't wait around for you, anyway. He's a lost cause. Why would he buy the cow when you already giving him plenty milk? I don't know where you getting your relationship advice from. You ain't never seen me or any of the peoples I deal with carry on in such a manner. Plus, how you think he gonna take care of you? The boy ain't never done a hard day's work in his life. Look at his hands. They soft as a baby's bottom. I don't know what to say about your judgment, Mary."

Mary had ignored her momma every time she started yelling about what Travis was not going to do for her. She used to dream of Travis before she met him. The man in her dreams was not named Travis; he was not named at all. He was a tall, brown-skinned fellow with well-defined features and fine thick hair. Big brown eyes were set in a baby face with a natural, perfect arch to his brows. His eyes would see straight through her, knowing she needed him. He had what old folks called "woman eyes," — eyes that looked as if they belonged on a girl. Nothing else about him was womanly at all. Everything from his strong, tall, solid build to his deep voice and calm cool manners made her want to dream of him every night.

The first day Mary set her eyes on Travis, she figured God had sent her the man that had been visiting her nightly in her dreams. Just like in her dreams, she did everything possible to get his attention. Unlike her dreams, she did not have to endure the torture of him turning her down. Travis took to Mary the first time he saw her. Just like that, she started going against everything her momma had taught her.

Mary's reasoning for her momma fussing all the time was that she did not know what it was like to keep a man of Travis's nature pleased. Travis was nothing like her father. Mary's daddy was laid back, easygoing and easy to keep satisfied. Mrs. Tobert did not have to do much to keep him happy. All Mr. Tobert wanted was a hot meal when he arrived home from work and a clean place to lay his head. Mary reasoned that was simple.

Travis, on the other hand, needed excitement. He admitted he was a roamer. He said it was not one place that could hold his attention long enough for him to plant his roots. Many times he told Mary that he was bound to leave Kansas soon as he had his fill. Said he was bound to go wherever else was calling him as soon as he felt the itch. He also mentioned he must have inherited the itch from his daddy because his daddy never stayed put. Months or even years at a time, his daddy would leave the family, eventually returning with stories about the places he had been and the people he had met.

One day, Travis told Mary that something in his bones was telling him to take her along with him.

About a month later, after they had had a night of the best lovemaking he had ever given her, he suddenly pulled her on top of him, looked her in the eyes and yelled out, "Florida! Florida is where we gonna start our lives together."

At seventeen, it all sounded good to Mary. So, Florida it was. Two years after they arrived in Florida, Mary experienced firsthand, the "itch" to which Travis had referred. When he began changing, she started dreaming of that man again. Mary prayed the man would stop coming to her in her dreams because she already had the man she needed—Travis.

With all her might, she tried to fix things in order to make Travis stop itching. She even suggested they go somewhere new. Well, he took her advice. He went somewhere new, without her.

Abandoned at the age of nineteen, she blamed him leaving on herself. Not only did she blame his leaving on herself, but she blamed herself for the baby dying.

It was not until recently that she finally admitted to herself that her momma had been correct. When she had tried calling her momma, the rejection she had received informed her that it was a lesson learned too late.

7

Cherry (Heather Lee Witman)

Y ou like being black but looking white?" the short, stout, white,
blond-headed man questioned Cherry.

"I mean," he stopped to wipe the sweat from his
forehead before continuing, "if nobody had of told me, I would have
sworn you was a red-blooded American. You's a real pretty girl.
Real pretty."

He looked at the ground when he spoke the last two words.

"Why you fooling around with the likes of these porch
monkey whores? You live with 'em like they normal people. You
don't belong in that house. If you moved away, a man could make
you an appropriate wife."

Cherry looked over at Marcus Huckenberry and took a deep
breath before speaking. Even though it was not noon yet, she had
already gulped three glasses of bourbon and was not in the mood for
his retarded ass. She could not figure Marcus's family out. Why they
allowed him to roam freely did not make sense to her. He was a full-
grown man, but acted more like a teenager. Though he was short,
about five-foot, he had a scary strength about him. "Retarded strong"
is what people called it. Marcus's left hand was gone. There was a
small nub in the place where a hand should have been. Cherry had
learned he had been born like that. The lack of a hand made him lean
to the left side when he walked.

"Marcus," Cherry finally spoke. "Don't matter what I look
like, we both know what I am. If you think all these women who live

in this house is porch monkey whores, well, then you think the same thing about me. 'cause my momma resembled them more than myself."

"I wasn't calling you a porch monkey whore," Marcus said in an embarrassed tone. He rubbed his nub against his leg, as he did whenever he got nervous. "I would never say something so bad about you. I thinks you is the prettiest woman in town. You prettier than all the full-blooded white women who live around here."

Marcus got quiet and used his good hand to rub the nub. "You mad at me, Cherry? I don't want you be mad with me. I likes you. I like you a lot."

"You like me so much, then why don't you ever come visit me at night?" Cherry knew the question would make Marcus anxious. Anything that had to do with sex made him jittery.

"I couldn't do that!" he said, his voice changing. The sound of rage appeared. "Bible say you shouldn't sleep with a woman unless it's your wife. Bible say women like you will send me to hell. That's what happened to Adam. He listened to Eve and he had to suffer 'cause she tricked him. Eve wasn't a whore, but she wasn't right, either. She knew she wasn't supposed to eat that apple, but she did. Eve was wicked and full of trickery! You trying to trick me, Cherry? You trying to send me to hell?"

"No, Marcus I'm not trying to trick you." Cherry forced herself to hold her laugh inside. "I'm simply offering you what I offer all the men who spend money on me. Marcus, the only way you can spend any time with me is by giving up some money. You right about the Bible. We all ain't blessed to be able to live by it. But if you did decide to sin, God would forgive you. God's a good man. He wouldn't send you to hell for having a good time. If you did decide to see me, you could easily have all them good people at your church pray for you and they would stop God from sending you to hell. Ain't there enough good souls in that church to save your one? I'm pretty sure all those praying people could save you."

"God ain't no man. God is a Spirit, a Holy Spirit." Marcus calmed down and continued talking. "Maybe I'll pray that you change. Maybe I'll ask the Lord to make it so you could marry me. He already made it so you look white."

With those words, Cherry let out the laughter she had been suppressing. "Marcus, you *real* funny. You go on ahead and pray that prayer. Even if I was to change, what makes you think your folks gonna allow me to carry they last name? They would just as soon see me hanging from a tree and you, too, if you tried to stop them. Now I bet that's one prayer them folks at that church of yours couldn't fix."

"They wouldn't have to know," he argued. "We could leave from these parts. Yo' momma did it. Folks around here say she left with a white man. You think it would be possible for us to do the same thing?"

Cherry got quiet with the mentioning of her momma. She did not mind talking bad about her momma, but she did not take kindly to other folks doing it. She hated hearing a retarded boy judge her momma's memory.

Taking a deep breath, Cherry said, "Marcus, I don't appreciate you speaking on my momma. You wanna stay my friend, I'd advise you not to mention my momma to me. You have never heard me say one thing bad about your momma and folks around here saying she the reason your hand is missing."

Marcus looked at the spot on his hand where fingers should have been. "Sorry," he mumbled.

Just then Madam Honey opened the door and, at the sight of her, Marcus scurried off. "You might want to be careful of that backwards fool," Madam Honey said, taking a seat in her chair on the porch.

"He's all right," Cherry replied, concealing the pain Marcus had made her feel.

"All right my big spotted ass! That boy is trouble. Marcus wants you so bad it's driving him crazier than the way he was born. He don't want you like a decent paying customer. He wants you like a husband wants a wife. My vision ain't as good as it used to be, but I can see it in his eyes a mile away. He so out of his mind about you, he didn't even need to lay on top of you before he fell. He must have took one look at you and decided he loved you. That ain't right. A man never has plans on loving a whore. The right way is to bed the whore, then unexpectedly fall for her. Poor idiot don't even have enough brains to do that. Go inside and bring me a cup tea."

Madam Honey sat on the porch trying to shake the ire that Marcus brought over her. She hated the fact that she could not keep him from hanging about her property. Of course she had spoken to Sheriff Jenkins about him several times, but the Sheriff had not paid her complaints any mind. Marcus was his third cousin so Madam Honey knew she did not have much control over the situation. If it had been anybody else she complained about, Sheriff Jenkins would have run them off but, with Marcus, he did nothing. He even offered to pay for Marcus to have a little fun with Cherry, but Marcus turned the offer down, running off screaming something about the Bible and burning in hell.

8

Chocolate (Judy Brown)

Knowing Toni had left the room, Chocolate slowly opened her eyes. She thanked the Lord for two things at that very moment. First, she thanked Him that Toni was not laying in the bed next to her. Even though they were sleeping under different sheets, she knew in her heart that they were too close. Second, she was grateful for last night. The night had been slower than usual. Nights like that meant she did not have to put in too much work. Sure, she came in and pretended to be tired, but that was just to keep Toni away from her. She was pretty sure Toni knew she was faking sleep, but as long as she accepted the way things were, they would not have a problem.

One thing that Chocolate was sure of was the fact that her mood change had nothing to do with Toni. Basically, she was sick and tired of the life she was living. The only reason she did not pick up and leave was because she had nowhere to go. Once, last month, she had actually packed her bags and planned to leave. She had convinced herself that with the money she had saved, she could start all over somewhere fresh; start all over where her name would be Judy Brown or Ms. Brown, with perhaps the possibility of becoming Mrs. Somebody. What had stopped her before she made it out of the room was fear. It was overwhelming apprehension that had made her unpack her clothes and go down to lunch, pretending that the life she was living was okay, pretending that sleeping with stray men, married men and drunken men was a way to make a life.

It was this very life that had led her into a relationship with Toni. Chocolate had no previous intentions of loving a woman. Never before in her life had she even considered it was possible for two women to please one another. Toni had changed all the ideas she had grown to believe.

First off, Toni's only aim in life was to be happy. She never talked about a future that included leaving what she had or having nicer things. Toni's only want was a person who would love her and accept her faults. Change and pulling schemes were not a part of her plan. She was happy with Madam Honey's house and she learned to deal with the mess that came with it. Toni figured this was the life that was given to her. It was not the best life, but she had seen and heard of worse.

Toni was the only person around Chocolate who made any sense. Her conversation was real and never concerned money, men or trickery. She spoke about life and living. She noticed how deep the red color was on the roses that grew in the front yard and repeated the colors of the rainbows that formed after a long rain. No matter how bad a situation, Toni found some way to get some good out of it. She was the only peace of mind around.

Chocolate had never intended to accept Toni in her bed. It was in the comfort of the friendship where love found a place. Well, at the time Chocolate thought it was love. It was not until recently that she had realized it was not. There was no way possible for two women to love each other. Toni could never give her what she wanted out of life. Chocolate wanted a family. Toni did not have what it would take to give her the baby she wanted to have, one day, nor could she stand in the church house and accept Toni's hand in marriage. She knew that one day she would not need to drink Madam Honey's poison. One day she would be able to carry a baby that attached itself to her womb.

Finally getting out of bed, Chocolate stood and stared at her reflection in the mirror. Her smooth, coffee-toned complexion was as it had always been. Looking into her own deep brown eyes, she thought of what she had heard her entire life.

'*She got her momma's eyes, but all else about her is her daddy.*'

Those words had always been said in a mean-spirited way. Then Chocolate's momma had died before she was old enough to remember her.

It was said by the woman who raised her that her mother was a bright-skinned woman with golden blond hair. Her daddy, on the other hand, was a good looking, dark-skinned man. After her momma died, he could not raise Chocolate, so he gave the job to a cousin of his. Being that the cousin did not care too much for Chocolate's momma, she did not take good care of her. So, Chocolate ran off as soon she figured her legs could get her away from the woman.

After spending a lifetime hearing how bad she looked, all on account of how dark she was, it was easy for Chocolate to be taken in. Madam Honey was not the first person for whom she had sold her body. The first was a man called Sly. Sly was something else. not be that bad.

He was real mean. He treated Chocolate like she felt inside—bad. Soon, she found out that he got more pleasure out of beating his women than taking money from them. When a whore told Chocolate about a lady pimp, she left with what money she had made that night and found her way to Madam Honey. She figured a woman pimp could

The minute she laid eyes on Madam Honey, Chocolate fell in love. All the loud talking and rules of the house did not detour her one bit. She even thought the name given to her by Madam Honey was cute, Chocolate. Having permanent clean living quarters was a plus. With Sly, she had moved from dirty motel to dirty motel. There were plenty of nights when she had made her living from the back of cars and on the ground behind juke joints. Madam Honey gave her a sense of family, an ease that had been absent from her life. Before Madam Honey, nobody had ever looked after her. Her father's cousin never spoke words of kindness, nor did she worry about her well-being.

It was now close to ten years Chocolate had been with Madam Honey. She had seen women come and go. But it had not been until now that she had felt an urge to get up and get out. When she had first walked through the doors, she had been twenty years old and thought she knew it all. Twenty years of confusion had walked into Madam Honey's house with her. At thirty, Chocolate now felt she had been tricked—tricked by nobody but herself. She understood she could not blame her state of living on Madam Honey because she had walked into her house and willingly had asked her for a job. Madam Honey had not promised her anything except safe, clean working quarters. No, Chocolate had been tricked long before she had introduced herself to Madam Honey.

9

Pretty (Saless Howard)

Pretty stepped lightly as she walked down the stairs. Not only did she always manage to sway her full hips from side to side in a seductive manner, but she carried herself in a pompous fashion. If one saw her outside the whorehouse, it would have been easy to mistake her for somebody with a meaningful title or position. She could have effortlessly fit into the role of a doctor's wife, the head of a charity board, or anybody of that nature. Her head was forever held in the air, as if to silently say she was of better quality than the others who resided at Madam Honey's.

For one thing, Pretty did not come across as a common prostitute. She did not wear skimpy clothes or cover her face with gobs of makeup. The only thing she did to enhance her appearance was add a light coat of red lipstick to her lips. As far as her clothing went, she bought expensive outfits, but they were never scanty or immodest. Whenever a man entered her room, her body was always well-covered. Once she was behind locked doors, and only then, she revealed what was under her long dress or the turtleneck blouse and long skirt she liked to sport.

The other girls were forever whispering about her "church outfits," calling her an old lady. They wondered out loud why somebody living in Florida would order a turtleneck blouse or sweater. Pretty just let these comments ride. She felt there was nothing to prove to any of them. As long as the men continued paying for her services, she would do as she pleased.

Besides, Pretty was very fortunate that she had a natural beauty, a beauty that did not require rouge, eye shadow, or a thick coat of eyeliner to enhance her eyes. She was exactly as her name said—pretty. Men referred to her as a "red-bone," which means a light-skinned girl. Actually, she was not so light that she could "pass," but she was light enough to make people wonder what other race her mother or father had mixed in their blood other than black.

Her long straight hair hung down to her waist. She took pride in the length of her hair. The fact that it was longer than most white women's sparked her confidence. Often she would laugh to herself as she watched the other girls come downstairs with an array of different wigs. One day a girl might have a short bob, while the next she appeared wearing a curly updo. Pretty never changed the color of her long, silky, straight mane. She always wore it pulled straight back, either hanging straight or with the ends loosely curled.

Pretty loved exposing the beauty of her natural features. Her big, mysterious, gray eyes, long thick eyelashes, and full lips were features she admired without even looking at herself. It was the rose-shaped mole she liked most about her appearance —after her hair, that is. The tiny mole opened and closed depending on the weather. When it was cold, the mole appeared as a rosebud on her face, but when it was warm, it opened up and looked like a little black rose. Since she had relocated to Florida, the mole remained open. It sat right above her lip, toward the corner, on the right side of her face.

Madam Honey loved Pretty's look the first time she set eyes on her. To this day, Pretty could recall the very words Madam Honey had said to her. "You sho' is a pretty thang; sure to be a money-maker. A man would gladly give his whole month's salary to feel those naturally soft-red lips pressed up against any part of his body. I needs to watch you. One kiss and you's liable to become some ignorant fool's wife. I been in this line of work for a long time and I ain't never ran across one such as you."

Madam Honey had let out a light laugh. "You even carry yo' self like you somebody with some status. Yep, a man would love to feel that kind of dignity between his legs. Look at all that long, pretty, straight hair." Madam Honey stepped closer and suddenly grabbed a handful of it. Pretty stopped herself from backing away. The look on her face told Madam Honey she was doing a bit too much because she quickly let go and stepped back.

"Just what I thought." Madam Honey continued. "It's all natural. I bet you ain't never put a wig on yo' head." Then Madam Honey saw the thick scar on the back of Pretty's neck that she had inadvertently exposed and said, "I see all this pretty done got you in trouble before," she said, referring to the scar. "I'm gonna call you Pretty, 'cause you got to be one of the best ones that has come my way."

Pretty walked through the swinging doors into the kitchen. "Good morning," she said in a dry tone. She did not even bother to look in the direction of her coworkers as they sat the table. She really did not think too highly of Cherry, Toni or Chocolate. Toni and Chocolate's relationship made her skin crawl. Unlike Cherry, Pretty chose not to associate with the other women who worked in the house. They would have easily allowed her to befriend them, but Pretty's actions made it clear that she did not want their company. Toni prepared Pretty's usual breakfast—a glass of ice cold water, two oranges sliced in half, and a slice of toast. Pretty lived on a diet.

Bringing her thoughts back to the present, Pretty figured, ' *I have had my share of female relationships. Besides, at thirty-eight* (she could effortlessly pass for twenty-five), *I am too old to be trying to make any friends. Holding on to a friendship isn't something I'm good at, anyway. Each time I thought I had found a real friend, the friend's male companion ended the friendship.*

All the friendships had ended the same way. She honestly did not understand why each friend blamed her for their men lusting after her. The female would portray she did not mind her lover admiring her beauty, then Pretty would find herself in some uncompromising position with the male and the friendship would end. Pretty reasoned that if the female truly wanted to keep her lover, she would have put a stop to the man flirting with her.

It was the disagreement with the preacher's wife that had led Pretty to give up on relationships with women altogether. The literal battle had left her feeling God did not care too much for her. It had been a tough one, had almost taken her life and had landed her in jail. During the trial, she had spent six months in the county jail until an old lover of hers who was a lawyer bailed her out and took her case.

The complete ordeal both puzzled and scared her to death. Pretty did not understand how a woman of God could try and take her life. She knew right along with the rest of the congregation that his wife had seen the preacher eyeing her during his Sunday morning sermons. For nearly two months, the preacher's wife sat in the front pew of the church and watched every Sunday morning and each

Wednesday evening, as her husband of over thirty years openly lusted after Pretty so badly that he could barely preach his sermons.

It was the night the preacher's wife kicked in the motel door that had made Pretty decide to stop having anything to do with women folk altogether. She had also decided to only fool with men for money. In that way, she would only have more than an earful of lies to remember come sunrise. The preacher's wife and her anger just about killed Pretty. Already crazed, the woman entered, swinging her hatchet all about the room. What Pretty did not understand was why she was the only one in harm's way. Hollering and cursing like Pretty was a demon, the preacher's wife yelled about Pretty's clothes as if her husband had not been the one taking them off. It had not been Pretty who had taken a special vow to the insane woman. She had never promised to love and protect the woman "til death do us part." The preacher had made all those vows. Still, it was Pretty who would be the one to suffer for the vows he had broken.

Before the hatchet incident, Pretty had not given a flying fig about the preacher's wife. He had told Pretty, "It won't be easy walking out on my wife. Though the church will be upset, I'm going to do it." He had gone on and promised he was going to leave his wife. He had assured Pretty that he did not want her anymore. After that he promised to make Pretty his wife.

Most nights while they lay in bed, the preacher complained about his wife. He said he hated her looks, her build, and the way she cooked. Pretty had laid beside him wiping away tears of laughter as the preacher called his wife a black oily seal. Just as he said, upon closer inspection, the greasy, short-armed woman did favor a seal.

Suddenly, all his feelings changed the moment his wife had come through the door of the motel with a hatchet. He had started screaming about Pretty being a witch and putting a hex on him. In his panic, he blubbered to his wife, "I tried to stay away from her, but the devil has been working overtime!" While his wife swung the hatchet like a lunatic, she agreed with everything he said.

No, things did not go as Pretty had expected they would. Instead, the preacher did not raise his hand in her defense. He stood right next his wife as she whacked Pretty on the back of the neck with the sharp blade.

Pretty did not recall much after that. When she did come about, she was handcuffed to a hospital bed and found out *she* had been the one charged with assault with a deadly weapon. Later, she found out that the preacher and his wife had told the police that they were the ones who had rented the room and that Pretty was the one who had broken in with the hatchet.

The story retold was that the preacher and his wife had somehow managed to get the hatchet out of Pretty's hand, but she had continued to chase after his wife. It was then and only then that the hatchet had been used against Pretty.

The owner of the motel, a longtime member of the preacher's church, cowardly went along with the story the preacher and his wife told. The only thing that saved Pretty was the fact that the jurors were deadlocked in their verdict. It was decided that if she left town, all would be forgotten.

Pretty left town and did not look back on her way out.

10

Lacey (Larry Brookman)

Stepping out of the bathroom wearing a long straight wig and a big, bright hot pink gown, Lacey said to Mary, "Hey, Miss Thang! I hear you sho' had yo' self a good first night. I don't know what you was doin', but I hear you had the men running to your room. You keep at it like that and you gonna run me out of business." Lacey spoke in the highest-pitched-tone his baritone voice could manage to tell where he walked to.

"Thank you," Mary said quietly.

"Madam Honey sho' did pick the right name for you 'cause you is a bit of sunshine. Look at you. You sho' is a tall glass of water," Lacey said, looking Mary up and down. "You pretty, too."

Lacey said his piece and walked down the stairs. He was about six-nine and a solid two hundred and fifty-something pounds. His skin was a dark walnut brown complexion. Mary soon learned that Larry never left his living quarters, which was the shed she had first seen when she arrived, without wearing one of his many wigs. The wig ranged anywhere from jet black to platinum blond. This particular morning Lacey sported a long blond wig with tight curls. His nails had been allowed to grow so long that they now curled at the tips. He was famous for his red nail polish. His fingernails and toenails always sparkled in the loud color. Once, Lacey tried dying one of his blond wigs the same loud color. Instead of pink, the wig had turned a weird violet hue. Lacey had a tight-fitting, sequined violet dress made and called it a day.

"Hey, baby," Lacey sang, taking a seat next to Pretty outside on the porch, kissing her on the cheek, leaving smudges of his lipstick. Actually, he was the only person in the house Pretty associated with, outside of Madam Honey. Lacey being a gay male strengthened the bond of their friendship. It was Lacey's sexuality that sealed the deal.

"Good morning, lovely," Pretty cheerfully said with a smile on her face.

"How did you do last night?" Lacey asked, smiling and batting his long false eyelashes.

"You know how the night for the Mayor goes. A lot of screwing and no paying. I guess it went well enough. Madam Honey was happy."

"I know. Ain't that something? But you know how it is." Lacey shook his head as he spoke. "We gotta travel the road the way it was laid out for us. If it wasn't for the one free night, we'd be getting busted every other night. One night of freebees ain't bad for a guaranteed year of freedom."

"Ain't that the truth?" Pretty said matter-of-factly.

"So, tell me," Lacey said, sitting his oatmeal and toast to the side, "has Jed still been paying to spend the entire night with you?"

"Not in awhile. He said something about a funeral up north. Said he'd be back in town in two or three weeks," Pretty told him.

"Why he staying so long?" Lacey asked biting his toast.

"Said something about his wife wanting to visit with her family. He made like he didn't really want to be gone that long, but you can never tell with men like him. I don't let it bother me."

Lacey could tell by the change in Pretty's tone that she was lying.

"You think he gonna carry you away from here? Take you some place people don't know the name Madam Honey and make an honest woman of you? If it happened to Violet, it can happen to you. He has that look in his eyes. The look of love, not lust. You been doing this long as me and you know the look."

Pretty let out a light laugh. "The look, you say? You paying attention to a look? Me, I see the ring on his finger. That man has been wearing that ring so long, you can see the indentation in his skin." Pretty whispered, "They been married twenty-four years."

"How long he been paying to see only you?" Lacey inquiring the length of time uprooted the tinge of pain that tried to root itself in Pretty's heart every time she thought of Jed.

"Since I been here," Pretty softly answered.

Then lost in thought, she sat quietly for awhile and thought of Jed's strong arms and solid chest. Images of the few times he paid for her conversation came to her mind. "Don't take your clothes off," he commanded her one night. "Just come and lie on the side of me. We got all night to toss around naked. I want to know a little more about you." Thinking about that moment, Pretty could almost smell the sweet scented cigar that he had held in the tips of his fingers. "What's your real name?"

Shaking her head, Pretty erased the thought of Jed out of her mind before turning and said, "Look, Lacey, I know what you getting at, but it don't make sense to get myself all wrapped up in the impossible. I try to look at life for what it is. I stopped dreamin' a long time ago." Pretty rubbed the scar on the back of her neck. "If you haven't noticed, I'm not like the rest of these whores who live here. Don't get me wrong. I would love to leave here with Jed, but the chances of it happening don't exist. I'm all right with the way things are between us. I didn't sign up here to find a husband. I signed up to sleep with other women's husbands, for pay. What white man, in this time and day, you think he gonna leave his wife of twenty-somethin' years for a black whore? Bein' pretty don't mean everything. Sometimes it just means havin' a whole lot of fun if the man can afford it.

"It's safe here, Lacey. That's the one and only reason I took Madam Honey up on her offer to reside here. The last thing I need is to leave here thinkin' some man is gonna take care of me. The only men that have ever taken care of me are dead—Franklin and Washington. We both done seen what happens when a girl leaves here with thoughts in her head concerning love."

"Not all return," Lacey said with a mouthful of oatmeal.

"The smart ones never leave," Pretty whispered.

11

Chocolate (Judy Brown)

We need our own space," Chocolate said. She waited for a response from Toni, but none came. Chocolate knew Toni was not asleep because her breathing pattern was too fast. When she was asleep, she had a slow loud breathing pattern and the one Chocolate was listening to was quick and low.

"So, are you going to keep pretending you don't hear me!?" Chocolate had not intended on getting angry. She had no intentions of shouting at Toni. The blaring voice that filled the room was a surprise to not only Toni, but also to herself. She had rehearsed this conversation a million times in her mind. The break up was supposed to go smoothly. Toni was supposed to understand.

"We cain't keep playing like there is something there. We cain't keep living life sleeping under separate sheets!" Chocolate gathered her control and lowered her voice. "I'm tired, baby, and I simply refuse to do it any longer."

Toni never opened her eyes because she felt death in the room.

'*Why should I open my eyes to witness my own demise?*' she thought. Death required darkness and since she was already in a state of darkness, she felt it best she remain that way. An old pain overtook her entire being. An aching she thought had been forever erased once Chocolate had held her hand in public.

'*My 'somebody' has disappeared,*' Toni thought.

Toni's breathing quickened and she found herself doing something she had not done in years, at least not since she had taken on the role of a man. Toni found herself crying. She wanted badly to stop acting like a woman. To her, women and weakness were the same thing. With her transformation into a man, tears and such were supposed to have become part of her past. The morning she had put on a pair of slacks and Stacy Adams was the morning that her tears were to be shed in private. Toni was sure men cried, but she had never witnessed one in the act. Desperately, she wanted to suck it up and pretend that Chocolate dismissing her was not all that bad. The harder she tried to stop the crying, the louder the sound became. Stuffing the sheets in her mouth, she tried to muffle the hurting sound.

"I'm sorry." Chocolate's voice broke through the hurtful noise that filled the room. "Please don't think it's you. It's not you. It's me and the baggage I carried into the relationship."

Chocolate turned to Toni and wiped the stream of tears that flowed from her eyes. "You are the last person in the world I want to hurt, but I gotta deal with me before I can go on pretending with you."

Toni never spoke a word. Eyes closed and face soaked with tears, she did not even look Chocolate in the eyes when she spoke. She remained in the sanctuary of her gloom. To her, Chocolate abandoning her meant she would return to the world a lone outcast. Toni knew her situation was different than Lacey's. Men would always sneak around back to give him the company he so desired. Things for her were not that easy. A woman would never venture to Madam Honey's house requesting her services. The world simply was not created like that. She would have to wait until the women who lived there became curious and approached her. Most often, it would only happen a few times, and then she would return back to her life of loneliness. Always, the women blamed the incident on the drink or the moment. No one, except Chocolate, had ever accepted what had happened between the two of them and made something out of it. Toni knew there was nothing she could say to make Chocolate understand how significant she was to her.

12

Mary Ann Tobert (Bit-of-Honey)

Nervously, Mary sat on the edge of her bed. Tonight was the first night of her new beginning. In her mind, last night did not count. Yesterday she had been drunk and could not recall what had taken place. She had decided she did not want to become what Cherry was—a drunk. Cherry was nice enough, but Mary noticed that she lived in a state of intoxication, forever slurring her words and stumbling around the house. Evidently, she was such an alcoholic that she had to have a drink before breakfast. Mary figured the men enjoyed Cherry for her European looks as much as for her lack of intelligent conversation.

Not wanting to end up like Cherry, Mary made the decision she would try to go at it sober. She was not looking to get any pleasure out of walking into the situation wide-eyed. It was something about not knowing what she had done the night before that bothered her. Everybody in the house had complimented her on how she had handled the men. This bothered her since she had no recollection as to how she had handled them. Her momma had always instructed her, "Know what you are getting yourself into." No, she had not listened to her momma the first time around, but this go at it, Mary was determined to take her momma's words to the grave.

Taking a deep breath, Mary slowly drank the ice water sitting on the end table next to her bed. The slow jazz tunes floated up the stairs along with the smell of greens, baked chicken, mashed potatoes and brown gravy, yams, dressing, meat loaf, apple cobbler and fried apples. The strong aroma of the food made Mary wish she had taken that extra piece of meatloaf Toni had offered her earlier. Standing, she walked over to the mirror to check her reflection. In silent appraisal, she stood staring at her tall, shapely, half-naked, bronze body draped in a thin, see-through garment.

"Do I know you?" Mary asked the strange person in the mirror. "Well, it's high time we got to know each other. Whore!" The word came out of nowhere. Mary had repeated the word in the mirror five times. Each time she had said it, a different emotion took over her spirit. All but four of the emotions were hurtful. It was not until she had said the word the fifth time that the pain ceased. The third time had been the hardest. That third time Mary had to fight the tears from coming to her eyes. When she said it the fourth time, a new acceptance appeared in her eyes and by the fifth time she said it, the situation was settled. Without a drop of liquor in her bloodstream, Mary took on her new role. With all her emotions in place, she gathered her strength and headed down the stairs.

"I see you made it downstairs," Cherry said, slightly drooling and slurring her words.

"Yes, I got it together," Mary said with a slight smile on her face.

"You don't have a drink," Cherry said, looking at Mary's empty hands.

"I'll get you one," a tall, nice looking man interrupted. He was dressed in blue jean overalls and had the appearance of a hard worker. His light complexion and friendly smile made Mary feel at ease. His mannerisms reminded her of her father.

"Make it an ice tea," Mary said in a calm voice that surprised her.

"Just ice tea? the man asked.

"Do I sound confused?" She raised her eyebrows in a serious manner and batted her long natural lashes.

Back in her room, as the stranger sat down on her bed, he asked, "You new at this?"

"Naw," Mary said in a teasing tone. "Don't flatter yourself. You not going to be teaching me how to have sex. I've done it quite a few times before I was introduced to you."

The man let out a hearty laugh. "I like the facade you put up. It's kind of cute. I hate to inform you, but it's not working. I know women of your kind and you don't fit into the mode of the *regular* working girl."

Mary slipped out of the slight piece of garment, then stood before the man looking like a creation by Leonardo Da Vinci—a tall bronze goddess. Her soft, flowing hair hung over her shoulders and an innocent smile appeared on her face. "You're not here to analyze me. You are paying good money to fuck me. All this talking is wastin' time. When we are done, I'm lookin' to find another man who is willing to pay for my services, not conversation. So, Mr. Light-Skin-Green-Eyes, save the talking for somebody you visit during respectable hours."

Mary walked toward the man and pushed him down on the bed.

'*I like this power*,' she thought as she straddled him. '*I like being Bit-of-Honey*.'

13

Toni (Rainie Holloway)

Toni sat out back gazing into the forest. Her perception of life was confused since Chocolate had informed her that their relationship was finished. She did not deem it fair for Chocolate to snatch the comfort and peace of mind that completed her happiness. In the blink of an eye, her life had been completely re-tailored. The comfort that Madam Honey's house had once provided had been taken away.

She knew Madam Honey's house held a special tranquility for her. But just being able to live there and not be picked on was not enough. Chocolate's love was the icing on the cake that had made living in Madam Honey's house comforting. It was at Madam Honey's house that Toni had begun to shave her head bald. There was no particular reason that she could recall. A week after living there she had just woke up and cut off all her hair. Before the shaving, she had worn her hair pulled back and tucked under a Panama hat. She had what people called a good grade of hair. It had been long, reddish-brown, and had a natural wave to it. Her hair had complimented her deep, reddish-brown complexion. The few folks who had caught sight of it had always marveled about how nice it looked.

"Why you always hiding that pretty hair of yours?" Madam Honey asked one morning when she stepped into Toni's room without knocking.

"It's too much to deal with," had been her response as she quickly placed the hat back on her head.

Toni had never felt the hair belonged to her, just as she had never felt her body belonged to her. As long as she could recollect, Toni had wanted to be boy. As far as she could remember, she could always run as fast or catch a ball better than any boy on her side of town. She had even found herself looking at girls just like the boys.

Until she had moved into Madam Honey's house, Toni had felt out of place in the universe. It was this mysterious "something" tucked away in the forest that gave her liberty—the freedom to wear pants every day, the freedom to walk about in men's shoes, even the freedom to look women up and down and wink.

This location had even given her the freedom to shave her head bald. It was this same place that had allowed Chocolate the independence to enter Toni's bed. Now, she felt she had been pushed back into a box. With Chocolate leaving, her heart was placed in a dark room with no light or air. She recalled losing her breath when she had heard Chocolate explain to her that the relationship— their relationship, was no more.

Toni felt that everything needed light, wind and love in order to grow. Hearing such harsh words had made her wonder if was she going to die. At that moment, she had felt she as if she was being executed. Chocolate had introduced her to a slow painful death. All the happiness and togetherness Chocolate had allowed to come out of her died with the words explaining that what they had was now over.

Thinking things through, Toni could not comprehend why Chocolate could want such a beautiful thing to end. They had been in love. She had loved Chocolate not simply for the pleasures she gave her in the evening, after all the men had misused and abused her body, but had loved Chocolate the most for her mind. She had listened to her dreams, her wants and her desires. Up until the demise of their relationship, Toni thought she had known Chocolate. She had actually thought she was everything Chocolate desired.

Toni had realized something had changed or gotten in the way of their communication. What she did not know was that the change would lead to the end of their relationship. She honestly had thought Chocolate was going through a phase, a moment in life when a person has to deal with problems alone. Many nights, Toni thought about snatching the covers off of Chocolate and forcing her to love her the way they had always loved one another. In the end, she had decided against forced love. Forced loved never accomplished anything. It was forced love that had hurt her years ago. No, Toni reasoned. Forced love was never good.

Instead, Toni decided she would wait, allowing Chocolate time to figure her problems out on her own. But the way Toni saw it, the given time had only made her leave. Now, she was stuck with living under the same roof as the woman she worshipped. Leaving was not an option because she had nowhere else to go. If she was ever to step off Madam Honey's porch, she knew she would have to go back to being Rainie. Of all the confusion she had dealt with in her life, knowing she was Toni was an absolute. Rainie was the name that had been given to her by the people who did not understand her. Toni was the name that had been given to her by the only woman who had ever understood her—Madam Honey.

"How you holdin' up?" Madam Honey asked, interrupting Toni's deep thoughts.

"I'm all right. I'm pretty sure I'm gonna be fine."

Madam Honey pulled a chair next to her. The look on her face expressed a deep concern for the hurt woman. "Well, I know you gonna be fine. I'm concerned about how you feelin' at this very moment, though."

"You think she done fell in love with a man? You think maybe she messed around and believed some of the bullshit he fed her while he was payin' to lay up with her?" Toni asked.

Silence took its requested place between the two women. Madam Honey did not know how to respond.

"Men have always mistreated me," Toni continued. "The only time I got along with the opposite sex was when I was little, before my momma started fixing up my hair. Long before I sprouted breasts and my hips spread out. I know you cain't see much 'cause I dress so that my figure ain't exposed. Before I hid myself, three men took advantage of me. It happened right around the time that I talked myself into being a girl. I know you think it's crazy—me deciding to be a girl. Madam Honey," Toni turned to face the heavy woman, "I never felt like a girl on the inside, but I decided I was gonna stop being a tomboy and stop looking at girls the way boys look at them. I can recall it like it was yesterday.

"I call myself sneaking out. I put on a dress. It was a nice dress, a little short for the time I was living in, but it was nice. I combed my hair real nice like. Instead of pulling it back in a ponytail, I combed it straight down my back. I even put a few curls in it. You should have seen me. I was pretty. I even put on a little makeup. Wasn't much...a little pink lip liner and some eye shadow.

"Henry Philips and I were gonna have a date, my first date. I was about fifteen. I was gonna try this girl thing out, see how it fit me." Toni got quiet. Her voice started trembling. She told herself she was not going to cry. Chocolate making her expose female emotions was enough. Clearing her throat and letting the morning air dry the tears that tried to form, she continued. "Before I could make it to Henry, three boys from my school caught me on a dirt road and raped me. It was all blamed on me. I should have known better than to be wearing such revealing clothing and all that makeup." Toni turned and faced Madam Honey with a clear voice and dry eyes. "In other words, I was asking for it."

"We all got our reasons for the way we is today. My job isn't to question any of you. I simply take you in. You? I knew you wasn't gonna be like the other girls. I knew I couldn't expect you to carry your load by sleepin' with men. I also knew you had no place else to go. You couldn't even cook till I sat you down and explained the reason man created pots and pans. I figured I needed to create a reason to keep you around. You know that ain't like me. Generally, I deal in dollars. But somethin' in your eyes told me you needed me in a bad way. I ain't gonna lie. I thought a little weird about you. Who could blame me? You steppin' through my door wearin' overalls and a man's hat, and with all that pretty hair tucked under it. It was the look in your eyes, though, that educated me that you needed placin'. So I told myself, I'd place you here as a cook. You turned out to be a good cook.

"Baby, I'm not quite sure why Chocolate decided to transform the situation between the two of you. I do know one thing. I know it wasn't the love of a man. Chocolate is searchin' for somethin'. She always been searchin' for somethin'. I guess all young folks is that way. I can recall a time when I was on the hunt. Chocolate is different. I don't see no peace in that chile. She's not like the others around here. Seems to me all the happiness she conjures is mimicked.

"I know you've never noticed it 'cause you was on the inside. Me? I'm on the outside looking in and, from my view, I see more. I don't claim to know everythin', 'cause I have no idea exactly what she's searchin' for. She's a restless spirit. You, my friend, you were fillin' a space in her life. She never loved you. You were simply somethin' new, somethin' excitin' in her life. Me, myself? I think she enjoyed the whispers that went along with the relationship. I don't think she was doin' it on purpose. I think she simply didn't know any better. If she could have, she would have loved you. Look around. Not many people in this house love themselves. Most of us are livin' our lives fightin' demons.

"I know all this, but even I refuse to change. We all got our reasons. Greed be mine. I'm not ashamed to admit I love me some money. I figure I'm too old to be searchin' for love. I missed that boat. So might as well buy me some nice things before I leave this side of creation. Ain't much else I can do in my old age. Without a man, I have two choices—wash the stink out of some white woman's clothes or sell some ass. I voted along with the rest of my boarders.

"You, I worries about. I know I have a difficult end to my life. I fear yours is gonna be worse off than mine. You gonna have to put those thoughts of Chocolate up and focus on what you intend to do with yo' self. I know the nights seem long without her, but believe me when I say, time is runnin'. Time won't be waitin' around for you to feel better. Time don't give a damn about yo' feelings. You waste too much time hurtin' over what was never yours and you gonna look up and see wrinkles in your reflection.

"Seems like yesterday I was believin' the lies Rufus Smith told me about makin' me his wife. That man was finer than the hair on a newborn's ass. He was about my height with a pair of ebony eyes that every woman in town wanted to look into. I was young and he was slick. I bumped my head more than a few times tryin' to make things work for us. After awhile, I got tired; that and he ran off with a blond-haired, blue-eyed young white girl. I hear they went off to Paris. In Paris, black men and white women can make a life. I used to blame myself. All that seems like yesterday, but it wasn't yesterday. It was a hundred pounds and clear skin ago. Chile, it was a lifetime ago. I know you cain't imagine it, but Madam Honey use to be fine." A smile appeared on her face as she reminisced about her better days.

"It's probably best she cut you loose. Now you can start savin' yo' money, 'cause you was spendin' too much on her black ass, anyhow."

Toni had to laugh at Madam Honey's last statement. Even though the truth hurt, the comedy took a lot of the sting out.

"I don't expect you to stop lovin' her in a day's time," Madam Honey continued. "I don't think the pain ever leaves. I still find myself missin' the sweet lies and good feeling Rufus put on me, but I moved on. All we can do is learn from our life experiences— the good ones and the bad ones. I'm not tryin' to change who you have become, but it would do you some good to get past those three boys takin' yo' womanhood. Let your hair grow out. Put on a nice dress. Allow some of these men to spend some money on you. I'm more than sure I can find me a new cook to replace you. I'm not known for tellin' lies, so don't think I'm gonna start with you. Believe when I say, ain't nothin' Chocolate can do to you in the bed that a man cain't do, plus a little more. What those boys did to you on that dirt road was horrible. None of what happened was your fault. But believe me when I tell you, had Henry gotten to you first, you wouldn't be the woman you are today. You would have stayed the girl you transformed into when you set out to meet with old Henry."

14

Lacey (Larry Brookman)

Lacey sat in the chair next to his large bed. The wood shed that had been transformed into his room looked nothing like the compartment it had been built to be. It was a design that was before its time. Lacey's palace was soaked in pink and white designs. He had the print made especially for his taste. Martha Newman, a seamstress who often made his clothes, assisted him with the decorations. She even went so far as to dye the wallpaper to match the bedding. Three pink stuffed animals were placed in a corner against his dresser. All three were gifts from Mr. Magic that had been won at the town's once-a-year carnival. Mr. Magic took his family every year. The first, an enormous pink bunny rabbit, was received four years ago. The other two smaller rabbits had been given to Lacey a year later.

Thoughts of Mr. Magic brought both ecstasy and remorse to Lacey's heart. The fact that they were two men prevented them from loving each other openly. Unlike Toni and Chocolate, they had to keep their relationship a secret in Madam Honey's house. They would never have been allowed to sit close to one another in the open. Mr. Magic was not even permitted to walk through the front door and request Lacey's services. He had to sneak in through the back.

The knock on the door interrupted his thoughts. "Come in," he instructed in the rough, womanly-pitched tone he always tried to emulate.

"You got a full house. Four men callin' on you. Word must be gettin' around about you. Three are regulars. The fourth one is a new fella, some colored boy who ain't from around here. Young. Real young. At least one of the youngest I done met requestin' your services." Madam Honey loved it when Lacey had a full night. She charged triple for his services. He might go two weeks without making any money, but when he was in season, he made twice as much as the girls.

"Did Mr. Magic sign up?" Lacey eagerly asked.

"Yep," Madam Honey said smiling. "He wants to see you. He'll be comin' last. I figured you want to spend the most time with him." She walked out of the shed and returned back to the house.

"Damn!" Lacey said to himself. He had been hoping it would be another slow night because he wanted to spend most of it with Mr. Magic. Knowing he did not have a choice, he told himself, '*I'll have to hurry with the other johns. The less time I spend with them, the more time I will have with Mr. Magic.*'

He knew he should be grateful for the three men paying to see him. In the beginning, Madam Honey had a hell of a time trying to sell him. It was not that men were not interested in his services. They simply worried about others finding out they were interested. Finally, Madam Honey set it up so that the men could remain anonymous.

They were instructed to come through the back woods and were never allowed to enter the house. Money was given at least a week in advance. Madam Honey always enlightened Lacey as to who would be walking through the shed door. With each customer, enough time was given for him to be far enough away from the shed, ensuring that each man would remain faceless. Due to all the secrecy involved, Madam Honey only allowed him a maximum of five visitors a night.

Lighting a cigarette, Lacey reapplied his plum-red lipstick. As he looked in the mirror, he decided that tonight he would sport his short, dark brown, Dutch Boy wig and his sparkling, white tight-fitting ankle length dress.

He did not bother stuffing his bra when he got dressed. Mr. Magic did not like him pretending to be a full woman. Though Mr. Magic enjoyed the makeup and all, when it came to Lacey stuffing and tucking, it upset him. Usually, he did not do anything to upset the man with whom he had fallen in love with.

15

Mary Ann Tobert (Bit-of-Honey)

Y ou sho' picked up on this lifestyle pretty quick for somebody who's supposed to be new at this." Cherry wore a big white T-shirt, and her flaming red hair was pulled into a ponytail. She had casually positioned her body next to Mary's in the bed. The girls lay next to each other like sisters. Glancing at the look on Cherry's face suggested to Mary that her friend was not feeling well. There was a soft, sickening look about her. Her usual pale face was paler than usual and her lips were cracked and dry. A light film of sweat covered her body, which gave off a tremendous amount of heat.

"What's wrong with you? You don't look like you feel well. Has Madam Honey seen you in this condition?" Mary asked, jumping out of the bed and rushing toward the door.

"She knows," Cherry replied. "I think it's my body reacting to the medicine she mixed up. I felt better before I took it."

"Well, what's wrong? Are you going to be okay?"

"I'll be fine in a few days. I messed around and caught one of those social diseases."

"How did you do that?"

Cherry took one look at the seriousness of Mary's face and burst out laughing. "You really don't know? Chile, you got a long way to go in this business. You looking at me like I'm on my death bed. I'll be all right. It happens to all of us at one time or another. It's bound to happen to you. It comes along with the type of work we do. You slip up and you get caught up."

"How do you catch it? That sickness you got," Mary asked.

"It just happens. It's part of the job"

"What do you mean it's part of the job?" Mary asked, puzzled.

"I was drunk, Mary. The same way you was the other night. It ain't like I planned on waking up sick. It just happened!" Cherry got control of her anger. "Sorry. I didn't mean to yell at you. I know you just asking 'bout what you don't know. It ain't as bad as it looks. The plus side is I gets to spend a little time to myself, resting up for the next time some nasty bastard gives it to me."

"Can I ask you something?" Mary said in a low serious voice.

"You can speak to me anyway you wish. Ain't much that offends me. I have been called everything but a chile of God. I know my place in this world. I'm used to pretty much all that has been laid before me," Cherry answered.

Mary asked, "Why you drink like you do? Why you walk down them steps in such a condition that you can get sick like this?"

Cherry took a deep breath before she spoke. A weakness Mary had never witnessed appeared in Cherry's eyes. Mary felt as if she was talking to a stranger. The person she had met on the porch steps, a few months ago, when she first arrived at Madam Honey's had all but disappeared.

"The pain I bear now is harder than the pain the folks in this house bring on me. My life is unlike most of the girls here. Everybody else in this house was running from something. They found Madam Honey and she gave them the something they were searching for. I'm not gonna pretend what they found was a good thing, but they were able to find a replacement for what is on the other side of Madam Honey's doors. Most of the residents who live here can speak of a past. I'm pretty sure you had a momma or a daddy that used to love you. Me? I ain't never had that. My whole life I was a burden to my momma. I never had the opportunity to choose what type of life I was gonna have. I was placed here. My momma gave me to Madam Honey."

Mary did not realize she was crying until Cherry took a handful of the sheets they lay on and wiped her tears. "You ain't gotta cry for my pain. I'm used to it. I'm not gonna lie and say it don't hurt. It's something I learned to deal with years ago. It's more of a discomfort than a hurt. Drinking dulls the feeling, but it's always there. But you make it a lot easier to live with."

"Me?" Mary asked in a bewildered voice.

"Yep, you. You allowing me to enter your room when I'm in this condition is helpful. They don't like me. They don't like me for the same reason my momma didn't like me. All on account of how I look—me looking like a white girl, but being a nigga. They see in me all the pain they living. In they minds, my features is the reason they are treated second class. You the first friend I have ever had. You are my friend, right?"

"Yea," Mary replied. "You're a nice person. I don't understand..."

"We don't all get to understand life," Cherry said, cutting her off. "As long as we understand us, that's pretty much all that matters. As long as we ain't confused like Toni and Chocolate are, we can make a good team. I ain't never understood why they would live the way they do. Still, I ain't ever called them on it. I figured as long as they is happy, it ain't none of my concern. Still, I don't agree with their sleeping arrangements."

"You got a point," Mary said, lying back in the bed next to Cherry.

16
Pretty (Saless Howard)

As she watched in fascinated horror, Madam Honey reached in between her large, saggy breasts and pulled out the small twenty-two she had tucked away. Pretty thought in a panic, *Oh, no, there she goes again!* Pretty jumped from the loud noise just as the body hit the end table before landing on the floor.

"Damn fool. His mistake," Pretty muttered to herself as she stepped over the corpse before heading to her room.

"Toni! Gone and get the Sheriff!" Madam Honey called as she replaced the still smoking weapon back from where she had had it concealed.

Pretty sat in her room, feeling both relieved and hurt. She was relieved because she would not have to deal with any men tonight. The murder would give all the girls an official night off while Sheriff Jenkins did a make-believe investigation. This would give the town's people something to wonder about as to what was taking place out at Madam Honey's whorehouse. She was sure a false article would be written up in the paper about a madman who had entered the house and attacked Madam Honey. The paper would use her Christian name, Abigail Richard. All the donations she made to the county, the homeless shelter, the school and the First United Baptist Church would be mentioned and the stranger's death would be overlooked. Pretty knew it was the money that made the town folks turn an eye to Madam Honey's line of work and the killing sprees that often took place on her property. She thought it was funny how they praised her cash, yet disassociated themselves from her presence.

"She went and did it again," Lacey stated, stepping into Pretty's room. Normally, he did not frequent the house during working hours, but with Madam Honey using her pistol, he knew the rules had changed for a short time.

"You know the routine. She was disrespected and he met his maker," Pretty stated.

"Same as always," Lacey replied.

Pretty did not even have to give an explanation as to what had happened. Lacey did not dig for details as he had witnessed enough of Madam Honey's rages to last him a lifetime.

"You have any customers tonight?" Pretty asked Lacey, trying to change the mood in the room.

"Naw. I was painting my nails when I heard the gunshot. I waited for the place to clear up a bit before I came in. Mondays are generally slow for me. I was wanting Mr. Magic to come by, but I guess I wasn't on his to-do list. He'll be in sometime this week. How about you? How did you do?"

"I turned three tricks before she went off and killed that boy. He couldn't have been no older than sixteen or seventeen. He might have been younger than that. I don't know, Lacey. That wasn't right. This time she overstepped her boundary. That was a baby's life she took. He just didn't look to be a full-grown man. That was plain wrong. I don't know how she's gonna sleep tonight."

"She's gonna sleep like she always does. In a large bed with satin or silk sheets. It all depends on what type she had Toni put on her bed."

"I don't know how she takes life so easy."

"Honey," Lacey said putting his hands on his hips, and using a matter-of-fact tone, "Madam Honey would sell life if there was an asking price for it. She don't give a damn about nothing but money. You gotta respect her for her honesty. She don't make like she gives a damn about anything other than greenbacks."

Lacey let out a rough, manly laugh. "Watch how they make her to be some respectable hard-working citizen in the paper. That's the only time she's referred to as Abigail Richard. Any other time, she's that fat, spotted whore who runs the nigga whorehouse. Naw. These folks around here don't like her. They just turn their heads while she's doing what she's doing. Matter of a fact, they hate her. It's her money that they love."

Lacey got up and walked toward the door. "I'm gonna go back to my place. Since I know it won't be no more working going on, I may as well soak my feet or do my nails. Wish I could go to sleep, but these working hours stay with you."

"See you in the morning," Pretty said.

17

Madam Honey (Abigail Richard)

Madam Honey sat on the porch eating hot cracklings and drinking warm buttermilk. It was early in the morning, so the heat had not yet set in. Killing the boy a few weeks back had stayed on her conscience. Caring about the life of somebody else, especially a stranger, was a different emotion for Madam Honey's train of thought. Usually, she did not think twice about taking a life. She figured that since hers had almost been taken without a second thought, why should she waste her time pondering about taking the life of somebody who she had never known.

Years ago, a john had beaten her within an inch of her life and had left her for dead. Since then, each and every time she got the opportunity to kill one, she had done just that. Black or white, it did not matter. The white ones did not get death, though. Madam Honey just called for Sheriff Jenkins and more times than not, the Sheriff would beat the hell out of them. That was all the satisfaction Madam Honey received when a white man disrespected her.

Today, the glory feeling she usually gained after taking a life did not meet her with the sunrise. Instead of feeling proud and satisfied, she felt bad.

"That woman gots to be part devil. She done went and shot that young boy dead," a voice echoed behind her.

Madam Honey turned to see who had spoken the words, but was met with silence when she turned her head in the direction of the voice.

"I ain't no devil," Madam Honey muttered. "I ain't."

Sitting on the porch, she was beginning to second guess herself. The boy's big, piercing ebony eyes would not leave her mind.

"He still had baby hair," Madam Honey said out loud. She remembered the blood caked around the edge of his forehead. His soft, naturally curly hair seemed to grab hold of the blood. No hair was on his smooth face. Madam Honey could not help but wonder if he had even grown his wisdom teeth. "A nice looking boy," she said out loud to nobody.

She sat on the porch by herself. Madam Honey reasoned it had not been her fault. He had stepped in her house and disrespected her in front of everybody. The boy had asked, "What's the going price for Pretty?"

She had looked him up and down and asked, "How old you be?"

In response, the boy had looked Madam Honey in the eye and told her, "I could pay what you be askin'. It be my money and not my age that matters," he had gone on to explain.

He turned and winked at Pretty before he continued. "Tell me the price and I'll give ya the money. That way you can take it and eat it up. The way you built, it looks to me that's where all the money goes, anyhow." Instead of a roomful of laughter, which is what he had expected, the room got quiet. It was in that dead silence that Madam Honey shot him.

"They heard him talkin' down to me," Madam Honey spoke out loud to no one as if still trying to defend herself.

Staring off into the forest, Madam Honey suddenly noticed a strange girl dragging herself through the trees. The girl headed her way was not pretty. As a matter of a fact, from afar, she was ugly. Madam Honey had to stop herself from laughing out loud at the child's features when she got a better look at the creature. She had buckteeth and baseball bat-sized legs with knees too big for the little sticks that carried her frail body. Madam Honey noticed the girl had a strange, sickening complexion. It appeared to be a chestnut brown covered with a film of white ash so intense it gave her dark brown skin a white coat. As Madam Honey cocked her head to the side, she noticed the poor sickly creature was also with child.

"'Bout three or four months pregnant," Madam Honey whispered to herself. "Toni!" she yelled as she watched the girl fall to the ground.

"Yes," Toni replied, running to the porch.

"You go get Lacey and y'all carry that girl in the house." Madam Honey pointed toward the direction of the limp body lying on the ground. "Hurry! She looks real sick."

"Where she come from?" Toni asked.

"Do as I say! I ain't got time to be answering no questions! Go get her now!"

18

Chocolate (Judy Brown)

I didn't know I wanted a child until now."

Chocolate was not sure where the words had come from. She had said them so she knew she had to have meant what she had just said.

"That's why you stopped fooling around with Toni?" Cherry asked, slowly sipping her drink. It was early in the morning, and the alcohol had not quite grabbed ahold of her senses. Cherry had had enough of the girls in the house looking her up and down. Since the break-up, Toni turned bitter and wicked— that is, until the wild pregnant girl had arrived.

Needing to be by herself, Cherry had decided to head outdoors, intending to have a drink away from the people who despised her for no reason. She would rather be around hate with a purpose. She felt the town bar calling her. In the bar was where Cherry intended to find the peace she sought. The women who shared a roof with her had no right to mistreat her, while the women outside of the house had plenty reason to hate her. After all, she *was* sleeping with their lovers and husbands for money that should have rightfully been kept in their households.

She would have invited Mary, but she was busy tending to the wild, strange sick girl, so she did not bother to ask her to accompany her to town. It had shocked Cherry when Chocolate had asked if she could come with her.

"I guess," Cherry answered, without knowing if she truly meant it. "Well, you have changed a lot since the two of you broke up."

"No, I've always been me," Chocolate responded.

"Before the break up, you would never have come to town to have a drink with me. Before the break up, you wouldn't have had a drink with me *in* the house."

"You think Toni had something to do with the way I treated you?" Chocolate looked in the glass as she spoke. "I mistreated you for all the reasons I was mistreated. It had nothing to do with Toni. Toni and I never spoke of you."

"What was the reason?" Cherry's voice grew angry as she demanded to know. The look in her eyes indicated she needed to know.

"Your color."

"Will this madness ever stop?" Cherry's voice questioned irately. "I wish you all would accept the fact that I'm black. I may have a little less pigment than you all, but I'm black."

"Why?" Chocolate never took her eyes off the glass. "Why you choose to be us when you could easily become one of them? It would be easier. Life would treat you better. Men would treat you better. I don't understand why you torture yourself. That's what you are doing. You mistreating yourself the way we mistreat you. Just up and leave. Find a place in the world where you can rid yourself of this life. There's a place in the world where people will respect you like a white girl. Hell, you can even work in a whorehouse for white girls. I hear the pay is better."

"Chocolate, please look at me when I tell you this. I need for you to understand my reasoning. That way you can go back and explain it to all the others who think I've got it better than them but choose to share the same misery they're forced to live with."

Chocolate slowly took her eyes off the still full glass of vodka and looked Cherry in the eyes.

"I loved my momma," Cherry said as she took a deep breath. "Don't get me wrong. I'm upset with what she did, leaving me and all, but I loved her. My momma was the prettiest woman this town ever laid eyes on and she was black. Not much black blood ran through her veins, but it was the black that made her so damn pretty. Look at me. Men think I'm so fine 'cause I look white, but they know I'm black. It's looking white but being black that gravitates all the men to my bed. They expect me to move different in bed, to sound different. I laugh at they silly thoughts, 'cause if that's what they want to believe, then so be it. Truth is, I cain't give them no more than what you can give them. I'm not all that pretty. I'm simply a black man's freedom to sleep with a white woman, while the white men who sleep with me, they a little different. I've come to the realization that they chooses me 'cause in they minds, I'm a little cleaner than my darker sister...I'm better. I suppose it's they horniness which leads them to forget that all those black men they look down on pay the same fee to have me. Chocolate, the same black men who sleep with you. Hell, when a case of the crabs breaks out around Madam Honey's, the damn bugs don't skip me 'cause I look white. Some men have false reasons for paying for my time. I'd be a fool to walk around like Pretty, feeling like I'm above all the other whores in the house, all on account of my looks.

"Now, my momma," Cherry downed the glass of bourbon before she continued, "My momma was a sight for any eyes, forget sore ones. Men thought my momma was so fine 'cause she was. I'm my momma's chile and if she was a nigga, then so be it, I'm gonna be a nigga. I'm not gonna act as if I'm somethin' different so I can be liked. All I got left of my momma is her memory and I'm not gonna throw that away just so a bunch of whores will accept me."

"I'm sorry," Chocolate mumbled.

"You don't have to be. All I ask is that you understand."

"But I do. I'm sorry. Cherry, I cain't recall my momma. She died before my memory could grab hold of her. I was told she was light complected. If I had been blessed to be able to remember her, I'm not even sure I'd have the courage to live like you. Knowing me, I'd choose easy. I always have. It don't do nothing but get me back to where I started, but I keep doing the same thing. Some folks call that insanity, doing the same thing but expecting different results.

"Sometimes I feel like God is playing with me. Take Marcus Huckenberry for instance. He ain't got a lick of sense. He was born that way. That's the way he's supposed to be. Me? I'm worse off than him. I know right from wrong. But I keep doing wrong. Why you think God let me live like this?" Chocolate asked.

"I ain't much on the subject of God. Best I can advise you is by telling you to go to church. We don't work on Sundays." Cherry motioned for the waiter to bring her another glass. "Church is the only place you'll find that answer."

"Them folks will run me out of church if I go in there asking them why I break Toni's heart when I knew I didn't want her in the first place."

"Why did you? I mean, I've always wondered why you would be with a woman. You could have any man you want. I'm sure you've had men want to make you their woman, you know like Pretty has. Even Lacey has himself a regular. He thinks nobody knows, but that house ain't big enough to keep walking secrets. But, that's not for me to be worrying about. It's the man's wife who has a problem. I don't get how two women could fall in love with each other. It don't seem possible to me. I've never been one to talk down about it. I've even defended it once or twice, but truthfully, I don't understand it," Cherry said.

"Comfort. Toni was the only somebody in the world who loved me."

"A woman ain't supposed to love a woman the way y'all loved each other," Cherry insisted.

Chocolate explained, "I knew that before I accepted her in my bed. It was just that Toni was the only *somebody* who cared for me with my clothes on. She didn't want nothin' from me. I couldn't believe somebody was taking an interest in me. Little ole' black me, with no strings attached. She's a good person. I wish she would change. If she ever started taking an interest in men, we could be the best of friends."

"I don't see that happening anytime soon. That girl is still wantin' you. I can tell by the way she looks at you. I know it's hard as hell for her to sleep. She's used to having you in her bed. What made you up and quit? You just cut it off and with y'all living under the same roof?"

"I'm not sure. I wasn't mad at her. She never did anything bad to me. It just didn't feel right anymore. Her being nice and tending to my needs wasn't enough anymore. Then it got to the point when all the attention she was giving me got on my last nerves. Her allowing me to ignore her revealed a weakness that made me sick. It was sorta like having a sick puppy following me around— a puppy that needed to be put down. Now, watching that baby grow inside that girl, I think it's 'cause I want me a baby, too. I want to raise my baby the way my momma would have raised me. I guess I figured I want to be a momma and Toni cain't be a daddy."

"It's gonna be weird having a baby in the house," commented Cherry.

"You think Madam Honey gonna let the girl and her baby stay?"

"Please," Cherry said, rolling her eyes. "The way Madam Honey tending to that girl's needs? The way she looks, I cain't see Madam Honey having her work in the house. That girl's been there two months and she hasn't spoke a word. She just lies in the bed staring at the ceiling. She don't take to nobody but Mary. That strange nameless girl's 'bout to worry Madam Honey to death. Any other time, she would have sent for the Sheriff to haul her off. Yea, that girl gonna be around—both her and her baby."

Shaking her head Chocolate said, "Any other time, Madam Honey would have killed that girl for spitting on her."

"That's the truth," Cherry said with a serious look on her face.

"It's gonna be strange having a baby live in a whorehouse." Chocolate's tone softened and a look of peacefulness appeared on her face. "It's gonna be nice though. We need something pure in the house."

"Let's go," Cherry said, standing up from the table. "It's getting late and I don't want Toni to think I'm the reason you kicked her out of your bed."

19

Marcus Huckenberry

You been hanging around that nasty whorehouse!" Dorothy's voice screeched at Marcus as he entered the house.

"N...n...no," Marcus stuttered and started rubbing his nub against his thigh.

"You a damned lie; a lie that's sure to go to hell! You been chasing in behind that fire-headed nigga girl. I keeps telling you she ain't white! Ain't a white girl living who would sell themselves to a black man! That girl is a jezebel. She sleeps with any kind of man for money! She's a carrier of social diseases! You not gonna be satisfied until she gives you something! You won't be happy until the doctor has to whack your peter off and you have to take a piss sitting down!"

Marcus kept his eyes on the floor the entire time his aunt yelled. He was deathly scared of the woman. It seemed to him that the older she got, the more her evilness increased. It was widely known throughout town that Dorothy would grab Marcus by his nub and beat him with the little black whip she kept in her hand or within grabbing distance. The one time he pulled away and stood up to the old lady, he had knocked her to the ground. Dorothy sent for Sheriff Jenkins, her second cousin. He came and nearly beat Marcus to death. He did not remember much about the beating while it was happening, but he did recall his aunt pleading with the Sheriff not kill him.

"I wasn't hanging 'round the whorehouse. I was lookin' for Cousin Sheriff Jenkins. He mentioned something to me about work. He said Madam Honey was gonna pay you good money if I did some yard work for her. I wasn't looking for that red-headed nigga girl."

Marcus had tears in his eyes as he pleaded his case.

"Good money, you say?" Dorothy's voice went from loud to soft in a matter of seconds. She knew the kind of money Madam Honey would dish out. She figured Madam Honey needed Marcus because not many women would allow their men or sons to be around the immoral place. "I don't want you back over that way until I talks to Sheriff Jenkins. I need him to assure me that you won't be pulled in by those nasty women and their lustful ways. You ain't got all your wits. It would be easy for one of them to take advantage of you. If that was to happen, I'd have them all arrested. I don't want them taking advantage of my only sister's retarded son, bless her soul.

"You recall how much money Sheriff Jenkins say she gonna pay you? Oh, you wouldn't know that. What type of work you gonna be doin'?"

"I think cutting down trees and tending her yard. I think Madam Honey bought some more land and is gonna build something else on her property. You have to ask Cousin Sheriff Jenkins to be sure," Marcus explained.

"I hope she ain't planning on expanding her unfavorable business 'cause the town won't stand for that. One whorehouse is a plenty for this town. It's bad enough decent white men spend their money there. Lord, I hope she don't want to build another," his aunt worried out loud.

"I don't know what her plan is. But I ain't lying. I promise you I wasn't running in behind that red-headed nigga girl."

"Go on in the kitchen and get you a bowl of beans. There's two big pieces of hot water cornbread on the stove and a bowl of dandelion salad on the table."

Dinner had been the same for the past two years. When Sheriff Jenkins was feeling kind, he would drop off some sort of meat. It was the starch that kept Marcus stocky; that and Dorothy passing up dinner every other night. Times had been hard for her ever since her father died. Marriage was out of the question. She had always worried that taking a man would mean putting Marcus second. She could not imagine a man accepting him and his condition as his own child.

Dorothy had promised her sister on her deathbed that she would tend to Marcus as her own. Lisa, her sister, had drank herself to death. Now Dorothy's sole mission in life was to make sure Marcus did not fall prey to the sinfulness of the world like his mother had. All the pleading and begging to change had fallen on deaf ears when she had spoken to Lisa.

Dorothy had plans to force the Lord into Marcus's life. Marcus took his first steps in church. The House of the Lord is where he learned to talk. She intended for him to walk the straight and narrow the rest of his days. A firm believer in the Word, she constantly reminded him that one day she was going to have to leave him; that she was going to go to that Great Glory in the sky and, after she left this earth, the only way God would look after him was if he was living right.

"I hope she's paying you enough for me to get caught up on the mortgage, the bank and all these taxes, or they is gonna be the death of me," Dorothy told her nephew.

20

Mary Ann Tobert (Bit-of-Honey)

Y ou all right?" Mary spoke to the girl as if she would answer. She knew full well that she had not spoken to anyone in the house since she had arrived two months before. Mary was the only one the wild child had tolerated being near her. No matter how nice the others had been, she screamed and spit when they approached her. Even Madam Honey's size did not intimidate the wild creature. The day she spit on her, everybody in the house stopped breathing. Involuntarily, Mary braced herself to witness what she had been hearing about—murder in the first degree. Her hypothesis was that Madam Honey was going to shoot the poor pregnant child in the head. Instead, she reached in the pocket of her house dress, pulled out a white handkerchief, wiped the warm spit off her fat chin and instructed Mary to help the girl upstairs. When Mary approached the maddened girl, she calmed down.

"Put her in your room," Madam Honey instructed when she saw how the girl had taken to Mary. As Mary approached her, she calmed her breathing and stopped kicking like a beast trying to attack.

Mary put an extra pillow behind the girl's head, handed her a glass of sweet milk and sat next to where she lay on her bed. Madam Honey had Lacey put a cot in Mary's room. The cot was for Mary because the girl had all but taken over the bed. "I put a lot of sugar in it this time. Well, I instructed Toni to put a lot in. It seemed to me that you liked it the last time it was made that way. I thought you was gonna drown yo' self when you was drinking it. You didn't put the glass down until it was empty," Mary said with a smile. The girl did something she had not done since she arrived at the house—she returned the smile.

"You have a pretty smile," Mary said, delighted that the girl was finally communicating with her.

Suddenly, the smile quickly disappeared and the girl put her hand over her mouth.

"You worried 'bout your teeth?" Mary asked. "That ain't nothing to fret over. Ain't nobody perfect. Pretty, the best looking woman in the house got a scar on her neck so thick it looks like a purple and pink snake is sitting under all that beautiful hair of hers.

" When you feeling better — and after you have the baby— I'm gonna fix your hair up real nice and buy you some nice clothes. You'll be amazed at how different you'll look with your hair combed. It's grown a lot since you been with us. When I get through with your hair and put a little makeup on you, your teeth will be the last thing men see. I'll be right back."

Mary left the room and came back with a bag. Inside were two yellow baby blankets.

"I didn't know what colors to send for. I don't know if it's gonna be a girl or a boy. Yellow is for both. When the baby gets here, I'll get the appropriate color."

The girl never said a word. She stared at the blankets for a moment, then turned and stared at the empty glass. "Oh, you want more milk? I'll be right back." Mary left the room and returned with two glasses of sweet milk. Another smile appeared on the girl's face and she quickly emptied both glasses.

"You look like you gonna be having it soon. I know you scared. It's easy to tell when a child is afraid. You don't look no more than thirteen or fourteen so your fear is written all over your face."

The girl frowned at Mary's remark. "Don't be mad at me for speaking reality. You supposed to be scared. If you wasn't, I'd be scared of you. A child in your condition with no fear is something to run from."

"For some unknown reason you pulling everybody to you. On account of you, we all speaking. Even Pretty been acting more sociable. All the conversation is 'bout your baby. I bet you wondering why a house full of women would get so excited about a baby. Well, we ain't regular women. We all whores. Whores are not supposed to be concerned with children. You helping us prove the world wrong. I guess we all gotta like you for that. I'm not sure how a baby is gonna fit in here with us, but we willing to make room. It's a new feeling that's floating around here. I don't know what to call it, but it's here. It's changin' this place for the better."

As usual, Mary continued her one-sided conversation.

"Madam Honey not attacking you when you spit on her was the first sign. If you ever get to talking, you cain't tell her I told you this, but she's a murderer. I heard about her before I got here, but I seen her in action not too long ago. Well, I didn't see her shoot the boy, but I saw his body lying on the floor— a little bit before you arrived, actually. The boy didn't look to be but a little older than you. She shot him dead 'cause he was talking down to her. I just knew she was gonna kill you when you spit on her. What I don't know is why she didn't. I try to tell myself it's 'cause you pregnant, but that don't add up 'cause the boy she shot was young. I'm pretty sure his momma thought of him as her baby.

"Chocolate believes it's 'cause Madam Honey didn't want to take two lives at once. I don't agree with that notion of thought, 'cause from what I hear, she done shot two men in the same night. To me, that's the same as taking two lives in one body. I don't know. What I do know is that you cast some sort of spell on the woman 'cause she's changed. She don't even mind me comin' late to work. That's 'bout as strange as you spitting on her and getting away with it.

"Madam Honey is serious about her money. Nowadays, she seems more concerned about you. She's always asking me about your health. The one thing she made clear was the fact that you need to get enough to eat. Toni is to make you whatever it is you want. If you was to open your mouth and say you want Hawaiian octopus and Alaskan trout, poor Toni would have to come up with a way to make it happen."

Mary stopped talking for awhile. Instead of making conversation, she did something she had not done since losing her own baby. She started humming a lullaby. While she was humming, she rubbed the girl's full stomach. The girl had been at Madam Honey's two months. Madam Honey estimated the girl was all of five or six months pregnant. All the hearty eating had transformed her small belly into a large round one. Madam Honey felt twins were a big possibility. She made the comment that the way her belly was positioned, it could be twins.

Mary was deep in thought concerning her own prediction as to about how many months the girl was along and humming, so she did not notice when the girl had first started humming along with her. She had wanted to ask the girl one of the many questions that danced in her head. Now, she almost fell off of the bed stopping herself from interrogating the poor child. Instead of asking questions, Mary calmly positioned herself back on the bed and kept humming.

'*She'll speak when she's ready,*' Mary told herself.

21

Toni (Rainie Holloway)

Toni slowly pulled the cap off her head and ran her fingers through the short, naturally curly, reddish-brown mane that covered her scalp. Glancing in the mirror, she acknowledged that she really was pretty. The morning she had awakened and Chocolate was not in her bed, Toni had stopped wearing the liner under her top lip. Even with the short hair that covered her head she had to admit she resembled a woman and an attractive woman at that. Still looking at herself in the mirror, she decided that, with a pair of earrings and some lipstick, she might even be considered beautiful. She was not sure why she decided to allow her hair to grow, but it was growing fast. No one in the house knew about it because she always made sure she kept her hat on whenever she left her room.

Keeping her hat on and staying clear of Chocolate were the two things Toni conscientiously did every day. Instead of worrying about Chocolate, she took to working hard long hours. After cooking and cleaning in the house, she helped Marcus in the field. The hard work made it easier for her to go to sleep at night. The first few nights she had been very restless—tossing and turning. Though she felt like crying, she fought the tears, refusing to let herself cry. To herself, she explained why she was not supposed to cry over Chocolate.

"She never loved you," she whispered over and over until

the hurt became as the rest of her life— a painful, yet acceptable, reality.

At first, Toni awoke in the mornings looking as if she had not had a wink of sleep— and most nights she had not. All the girls stayed clear of her, but the smirk on Pretty's face revealed that she was enjoying Toni's pain. In silence, Toni overlooked Pretty's ugly, smug grin. But deep down she pleaded for Pretty to make one smart remark about the situation. If and when she did, Toni had it in her to execute the bitch right on the spot.

It was not until the ugly, pregnant wild girl had arrived that Toni was able to let everything go. That night, she did not fight the tears. Surprisingly, after crying herself to sleep, she awoke feeling rested.

Toni recalled how she and Lacey had found the girl slumped on the ground. At first they thought she was dead because her body was so still and seemed lifeless. Suddenly, the girl woke up fighting. The first bite told Toni the girl still had life in her. When she had bent to pick her up, she had grabbed Toni's hand and bit it. Throughout all the punches and biting, Toni never lost her cool. Instead, she had managed to embrace the poor child, putting both arms around her. She held the fighting girl and carried her into the house with Lacey's assistance. But it was not until Mary had entered the room that the wild child had calmed down.

Finding the young, pregnant girl had helped Toni realize that she really was not defenseless or unloved. No matter how hard her life had been, she had never been forced to roam the woods pregnant. The lost girl had helped her to realize that God was indeed looking out for her. He was looking out for her in His own way. Also, she realized that Madam Honey, as wicked as she was, was also looking out for the young girl in her way, like not insisting she take men into her bed or just like she could easily have told Toni to let her hair grow out and get with the program. Instead, Madam Honey had allowed her the space she needed to be the person she was.

Inside, Toni was still that confused little girl who was trying to be a man. True, she had grown up physically, but her mind was still traumatized by the events that had happened on that dirt road with those three boys taking what the Lord had given her. The night they took her womanhood, Toni had decided it was a sign from God that she was not supposed to have it.

The night after she had found the wild girl, she laid in bed, letting the tears flow. After some time, she came to the conclusion that maybe life was not so bad, after all. Releasing the tears actually had made her feel better in the morning. It was the first restful night of sleep she had since Chocolate had moved out of her bed.

22

Marcus Huckenberry

Marcus hoisted the heavy log with his good hand and used his nub to balance the weight. He did not mind the hard work or long hours. In fact, he did not even mind that Dorothy got all the money for the work he did. As long as Toni continued to bring him buckets overflowing with exceptional tasting food, he had made up his mind that he would work for Madam Honey the rest of his life.

The first time Toni brought him lunch he had almost fallen over with delight. Before she had even arrived, he smelled the food. He stood watching as she hauled a bucket filled with both catfish and meatloaf. Marcus was pleased with seeing both meats in the bucket, but when he also spotted macaroni and cheese and cabbage, he almost passed out. In his eagerness he had almost forgotten about the bowl Toni carried until she sat it next to the bucket. When he lifted the handkerchief from over the bowl, he knew he had died and gone to heaven. The bowl was filled with cherry cobbler. The large hunk of dessert, with its golden-brown crust, was overflowing the bowl's rim.

That had been the first time in his life when he had been given so much food. Even during Christmas, when the church had its annual dinner, he had not been allowed to eat this much. At the dinner he had only been given a small helping of each dish and had to choose one type of meat he wanted. Marcus always wanted both chicken and turkey, but he never got them both. His aunt, at his elbow, always quickly reminded him that the other people also had to eat.

So excited that first time, he had to make an effort to calm himself before he began to eat the delicious food. While he ate, he asked Toni, "Can I borrow the bucket to take some food to my aunt?"

With a smile, she informed him, "You eat all that I brought you. Later, before leaving, I will give you something to take to your aunt."

As he walked home that day, Marcus was not sure if his aunt would accept the food. He knew how his aunt felt about the women living in the whorehouse, so he was not sure how she would respond to their generosity. Finally, he decided that if she started yelling, he would pretend the food was his leftovers.

Upon entering the house, Dorothy smelled the cold food through the greasy paper bag he carried. "What you got there? It smells awful good." The tone of her voice informed Marcus it was all right to tell the truth.

"Madam Honey sent it. She said it was the least she could do since you allowed me to work for her."

"A whore with manners. Ain't that something," Dorothy said with a mouthful of cold catfish. "She gonna be feeding you like this every time you go to work?"

"Yes. It's part of the work deal, me working out there and all. They sell food at night, so they have plenty. You don't have to worry 'bout fixing me supper. Also, you don't have to worry 'bout fixing you supper. Instead of throwing what's left out, Madam Honey said she would rather give it you since you allowing me to help clear her land."

Marcus figured it was best he keep reminding Dorothy that she was the one doing Madam Honey a favor.

"I guess she got a point. How long you think you'll be working for her? I mean, her feeding you like this, I don't want you to get spoiled. After the work is done, I hope you don't think you gonna be eating like it's a holiday on a regular. No wonder those men flock out there like birds heading south. I didn't know she fed 'em also. I was in the mind of thinkin' she was simply sleeping with 'em. They gets food and tail. If that ain't the best thing going. It's a wonder men ever return home. That Madam Honey is a slick one."

"I don't know how long she's gonna need me. I know I got a lot of work to do. One of the girls helps me out when she ain't busy in the kitchen. But a woman's strength ain't much."

"There's a woman out there that does man's work *and* sleeps with men for money? What kind of sickness that woman got going on out there?"

Marcus decided it was best he not reveal what type of woman Toni was.

"Well, as long as you being paid to deal with it, I guess I'll ignore all the madness. I just want you to remember what kind of people we are. We decent people. I don't think the Lord will mind you lending a hand to a group of whores. They were women before they chose that wicked life. I hope Madam Honey is grateful that I'm able to overlook all the evil she's got goin' on at her place. Only a strong Christian woman would be comfortable sending a man to deal with such nonsense. It's only 'cause you was brought up right that I'm able to do it."

Dorothy snatched the bag of cold food and went into the kitchen to heat it up.

23

Madam Honey (Abigail Richard)

Every morning Madam Honey made it a point to get up extra early in order to keep an eye on Marcus. Not bothering to get dressed, she jumped out of bed, put on a robe, tied her head with a rag and marched out to the porch to make sure he was working. Only when she saw that he was deep in work did she leave the front porch. The fact was, she did not want him anywhere near the house. She even took to instructing all her girls to sit on the back porch. The last thing she needed was for Marcus to get a look at Cherry and lose what little mind he had. It was explained to the girls that only in the evenings, when he was gone, could they return to the front porch. While he was working the land, they were to stay out back.

It had been Sheriff Jenkins' doing, insisting that Marcus help clear the land. Initially, Madam Honey had wanted no part of the simple-minded nitwit working on her property. Something about that boy scared her, made her nervous. His mind not being right was not an issue with her. Growing up, Madam Honey knew a lot of people with mind problems. In fact, she had a cousin who had been born slow. The cousin of hers had never learned how to control his spit or to form a sentence that anybody except his momma could understand. He went around slobbering all over himself and not talking correctly until he died in his late thirties. For some reason, Madam Honey was never scared of her cousin, as in her mind he was a normal retard. Also, she had never seen him lusting after women. He only did as he was instructed.

But Marcus; he was different. He had a look in his eye that scared her. The look reminded her of trouble. He was a problem that she knew she could do nothing about. If he was to lose his wits and go crazy over Cherry, she knew she would not be able to do anything but watch the insanity play out. Since he was related to Sheriff Jenkins, she was forced to put up with him and all his craziness.

Since the dead trees had become a fire hazard, Madam Honey knew they needed to be cut down. Two months earlier, Less Fisher had lost twenty acres due to a fire that somehow sparked up. It burned for five days before it could be brought under control. The county was enduring a serious drought and the last thing the Sheriff needed was his second income, which happened to be his largest income, to burn down.

Finally, Madam Honey reluctantly agreed to allow Marcus to work on the property. Though she did it with a smile on her face, what she really wanted to badly tell Sheriff Jenkins was that Marcus was not allowed anywhere near the house or her girls, especially Cherry. But as tough as she was supposed to be, she knew better than to give orders to any white man. Also, she knew his protection only went so far. Madam Honey's craziness was extended only to a certain extent. It all stopped when a white man walked through her doors.

Secretly, she would have preferred to keep them out. How she wished she could put a sign on the front door that read: *"Rednecks Stay Clear of This Colored Tail. We Don't Care for Your Cash."*

As it was, life was not set up that way. What she hated the most was what she needed the most. It was not that she hated men. It was more that she hated the power they had over her. In reality, they were only her girls because Sheriff Jenkins allowed them to be. Had he been some Bible-hauling ruler of the town, things would have been totally different for her.

The day the Sheriff got wind of what was taking place on her property, he came out and told her how things were going to run. He did not ask her anything. Instructions were all she heard. Madam Honey listened with the same smile she had on her face when he instructed her to allow Marcus to work the land and pay him twice as much as she would have paid somebody else. She even had to provide his meals and send something home to his crazy Bible-toting aunt.

Madam Honey did not think too highly of Dorothy. To her, it seemed as if Dorothy had allowed all the life to be sucked out of her. She was a small woman, who was shaped in such a way that one might think she was around twelve or thirteen. To this day, the woman was shaped like a little boy without any breasts or hips to speak of. Once you got past her body and actually looked her in the face, she appeared to be between ninety to ninety-five years old. Due to her working so hard outside, she was much darker than most white women. The sun had done her no justice, either. Her rough, leather-like skin and deep, wrinkled face accented the hardness of her appearance. If her teeth were not so rotten and broken in places, Madam Honey figured she would look a lot better. The thin, brittle, gray hair that covered her small pea-shaped head also added a lot of age on her. Madam Honey estimated that the woman had to be in her early fifties, but a person would have sworn she was lying if she stated that. Knowing women, she could tell Dorothy had probably been a decent looking woman at one time in her life—never pretty, but acceptable. It sometimes puzzled her as to why Dorothy had never married or had children of her own. Another thing that did not make sense was why she ran about after her dead sister's child. Madam Honey knew she loved the slow boy. She also knew she could have loved her own child just as much.

"Morning!" Marcus hollered as he came toward Madam Honey.

"What you doing up this way? I ain't got enough work for you to do? I ain't overpaying you to speak to me. I got plenty conversation in my house. I'm paying you to work. I expect you to do just that."

Marcus paid Madam Honey no mind and continued walking toward her. "Why you got a pregnant whore living with you?"

"Ain't no pregnant whore in my house." Though she tried not to show it, the remark Marcus made agitated her.

"Well, if she's living with you, she gotta be a whore and from what I see, she's getting ready to have baby. Who is she? I ain't never seen her 'round here before. Which one of the men who come to see her gonna take the baby in? I hope she know most of the men have wives at home. I hope one of y'all done explained to her that a whore ain't got no right to get pregnant. Why you think she let that happen? Why you think she went and did something so foolish?"

"Listen here, retard. I don't know where you got your information. That girl living in my house ain't no whore. She's pregnant, but she ain't no whore. It'd be best you mind your business 'cause if you think you gonna be snooping around here so you can return and tell that Bible-packing auntie of yours a bunch of lies, you got it all wrong. I'll send for your cousin and have you kicked off this place, never to return." Madam Honey's anger got the best of her. She did not realize she was shaking her fist at Marcus until she put her hand down to her side. Though she knew her threat was a lie, she also knew he took it as the truth.

"I ain't gonna say nothin'. I promise." Marcus then turned and hurried back to his work.

24

Pretty (Saless Howard)

Standing in the doorway, Pretty asked Mary who was sitting on the back porch steps counting the stars, "Did she ever say anything about the baby?"

The sky was crystal clear and the stars stood out like small neon signs. Counting the stars may have seemed useless to anybody else, but to Mary it kept her mind occupied. If she did not concentrate on something specific, her mind tried to dwell on all the things she did not want to think about. Lately, her mind had replayed over and over the day she had chosen Travis over her father. She finally accepted that her momma had not been wrong when she had turned her back on her.

Mary's love had been so strong that it had given her the courage to leave her father and mother for the man who had eventually left her.

'He left me for no reason,' Mary thought. *'All I did was love him.'*

Pretty's question had broken into Mary's reverie and she responded, without turning around, "No, she don't talk about nothin'. She mostly just eats and eats a lot. She like sugar milk. That child smiles when I bring her milk that has so much sugar in it that when she done drinkin' it, two inches of sugar is caked on the bottom of the glass. After drinking the milk, she takes her fingers and scrapes the sugar from bottom."

Mary laughed as she pictured in her mind a mental image of the girl scraping at the sugar. "No, we don't speak on much."

Pretty slowly began moving closer to Mary. She had just been getting used to Pretty being verbally social to her, but her being physically close was making her nervous. When she felt Pretty sitting right next to her uninvited, Mary began scooting toward the edge of the porch, away from the close contact.

For a few moments there was an uncomfortable silence. Then Pretty broke the tension in the air by asking, "How you stop yo' self from gettin' mad at her, Mary?"

"Mad?" Mary almost fell off the porch when she heard Pretty's question. "Why would I be mad? She's a child running from what I don't know. I know she's a child. I know she's scared. I don't understand why I should be mad."

"Well, I'm not really mad at her. I guess I'm more…." Pretty lowered her voice when she spoke the last two words. "Like envious."

Astonished, Mary said, "Of what? A girl who's so scared of life she cain't speak? That child must a done witnessed somethin' so horrible, it pains her to talk about it. Have you ever wondered how she's gonna raise a child without a voice? Right now, the last thing that speechless baby needs is somebody hating her 'cause she ain't talkin'.

"I don't get you, Pretty. You walk around here with your head in the air like God came up with a different type of prostitute when he made you. Now, you sit here and tell me you envious of an unwanted, mute, pregnant girl."

Shaking her head in anger, Mary continued as she looked up at the sky. "It probably been best if you had of kept things the way they were between us. I liked you better when you weren't speakin' to me."

"I didn't mean it like that. It's just that…" Pretty sat quiet for a moment. Tears swelled up in her eyes as she spoke. "I want a baby, too. I want a family. I don't hate her. I'm guess I'm mad at myself."

"Mad at yo' self for what?" Mary asked as she took out her handkerchief then wiped Pretty's tears.

"Well…I'm mad that I let all this time pass in my life and I don't have nothin' to show for it. Here I am, dreamin' of children and I ain't far from being a grandmother in age."

"Stop lying! You cain't be that old. You look better than everybody in this house. You even look better than Cherry and she's white. Not only do you look better, but you looks young. And as long as Mother Nature is comin' on regular, you can have a baby."

"I ain't got no husband," sighed Pretty.

"You don't see no rings on the mute girl's finger," Mary replied philosophically.

After hearing these words, Pretty opened up to Mary. For reasons unknown even to herself, she spoke of a topic she could not discuss with Lacey. In a soft voice she stated, "He wants to leave his wife."

Mary turned and looked Pretty in the eyes. Her look told Pretty she should remain quiet, but once started, it was as if a dam had broken. "He said he is willing to leave his family. They been married ova twenty years.

"I know what you thinkin'. I never brought the subject of him leaving her. Years ago I explained to him that he didn't have to make me any promises. I'm a whore and he's a married man. That's what I remind him of every time he comes to my bed. I don't question him about her. She's his personal life. She's his wife. It's not my place to question him about his family."

Pretty took a deep breath before continuing. She gazed up at the starlit sky and allowed the tears to fall freely from her eyes. "I pride myself on not carin'. I tried carin' before and it got me this." She turned slightly, then lifted her hair and revealed the thick purple and pink scar on the back of her neck.

Upon seeing the wicked-looking scar Mary wanted to respond, but for a few moments she could not say anything. Her mind just went blank.

'How do I comfort her?' she asked herself.

Finally, Mary commented, "You love him. You love him like I loved Travis...like you loved the man who made that scar. Pretty, you stay here and you'll end up like Madam Honey. Not carin' for nothin' in life. You almost like her now. Word is you stepped over that boy's body and didn't even shed a tear. Anybody who can ignore a life bein' takin' in such a terrible manner is probably 'bout dead inside. I'm not sayin' you should leave with that man, but I'm sayin' you should leave here."

"Oh, Mary, I know you right. I need to go. I may as well leave him here. I've got enough money saved to figure out my next move. I can find me my own husband. I don't need to take another woman's. Nothin' good came the last time I tried to. Nothin' good will come this time." Pretty wiped tears from her eyes and as she stood up gave a tremulous smile and said, "They don't call me Pretty for nothin'."

She paused for a moment then added, "I have no right to be resentful of a mute girl carryin' a baby. I got plenty time to have my own." Pretty then bent down and kissed Mary lightly on the top of her head. "I wish I coulda befriended you when you first got here.

You seem different. I'm more than sure you would have remained my friend."

Turning, Pretty resolutely went back inside the house and went upstairs to her room where she packed her bags and left through the back door. Glancing around, she did not see Mary on the porch. Taking a big breath and exhaling, with a bag in each hand, she marched toward the trees.

She had no idea where she was going to sleep that night. In her mind and heart she knew that if she slept in Madam Honey's house one more night, she might awake feeling as if the conversation between Mary and her had only been a dream. This could lead to her continuing with the life she had been living at Madam Honey's.

As she walked determinedly though the forest, she held her head up high. Pretty's life was over. Saless Howard was now stepping away from all she had ever known.

25
Mary Ann Tobert (Bit-of-Honey)

Madam Honey had been correct. The mute girl gave birth to twins, a baby girl and a baby boy. Sadly, the girl was born dead. No sound or breathing ever came from her mouth. Her small frame was limp and her lips were purple. Mary had to look twice to make sure she was not seeing things. But, no, she was not seeing things. That little baby girl had died with a smile on her face. Looking at that sweet smile did something to Mary. She closed her eyes in order to keep herself from crying, but it did not help. All the while tears trailed down her face, she felt bad as she felt she should not be crying over a dead, smiling baby. Her reasoning was that the baby was where it needed to be—in heaven. Why else would God have put such a wonderful sweet smile on the dead baby's face?

Placing the baby's small hand in her own, she lifted her to her chest. Turning to Madam Honey, Mary whispered, "She beautiful." Cradling the tiny infant, Mary tried to imagine what the child's life would have been like if she had lived. On the other hand, she firmly believed she was holding an angel—a little spirit that was too good for this wicked world. Turning the baby over, she actually felt on the baby's back for imprints of where a small set of sparkling white wings had been attached.

Turning the baby on her back, Mary gazed into the precious little face and imagined the baby girl opening her eyes. Silently, she wondered what color her eyes would have been. "Light brown," Mary said out loud. "They would have been light brown." She gently rubbed the child's head that was covered with soft, curly, light-brown hair, still tangled with dried blood and afterbirth.

"You think maybe her momma wants to get a look at her?" Madam Honey asked.

"Let her hold the boy. He needs to be fed. This one cain't eat nothin'." Mary never looked up when she spoke. Still holding the baby girl, Mary walked over and sat in a chair by the window where she slowly examined and counted to make sure she had all her fingers and toes. They were all there. The baby's small hands were relaxed. She had such long dainty fingers. Her delicate tiny feet hung freely from Mary's lap.

Raising her head, Mary commanded, "Send for Toni."

Toni rushed in the room with her head hung low. She knew the baby was not alive and the look of sorrow in her eyes said, "I'm sorry," but Toni could not bring herself to say the words. Even though she tried to look as if she was handling the situation, her eyes were red and her face was long. She gave up trying to fight the tears, telling herself it was all right to cry over a dead smiling baby.

Mary instructed Toni, "Go tell Lacey to let me borrow his pink nail polish. Not the hot pink, though. I need a soft color."

Soon, Toni returned with a bottle of soft-pink nail polish. The light pink color on the baby's fingers and toenails went well with the pink dress Martha, a local seamstress, made for the baby girl.

It was a small graveside service. All the women and Lacey showed up. Everybody cried except the preacher, who Madam

Honey had found in a nearby town. The local town's only preacher had refused to step one foot near Madam Honey. Therefore, she had paid for the preacher's traveling expenses, plus his stay at a boarding house while he was in town. He had refused to spend the night in her house.

The baby's death changed everything about the women. Dressed like ladies, not whores, the women all stood around the tiny casket. Toni wore a long black dress and a wig. Looking at her, Mary thought she looked pretty good, yet awkward. The high-heeled shoes she wore made her walk funny and she had on too much makeup. Still, Mary thought Toni looked pretty dressed as a woman.

Lacey transformed himself back to Larry. His tall, well-built frame looked quite handsome in the black suit he had Cherry purchase in town. For the occasion, he used his normal voice instead of the false high-pitched one.

The baby's death had caused the people in Madam Honey's house to reveal themselves in ways they had not before. Standing around that pitifully tiny casket, they were all equal. All of them so good at hiding their grief and pain, today, had revealed their true selves, something the speechless girl had been unable to do.

In fact, Madam Honey went out of character and stood up to Sheriff Jenkins for the first time since she'd known him. Mary overheard her telling him, "Ain't nobody gonna be workin' for a week. The girls all need proper time to grieve."

Peeking around the corner, Mary observed Sheriff Jenkins turning red in the face after Madam Honey's pronouncement. He was not going to take this from any black woman and with a blustering voice commanded, "They need to get back to work as soon as possible!" In his mind they had had taken enough time off as nobody had worked the day the baby was born and nobody had worked the day of the funeral.

Madam Honey looked him right in the eye and emphatically stated, "Nobody is goin' to work until *I* tells them to. Nobody is takin' any customers for another week!

"Knowing he had met an immovable force, an angry Sheriff Jenkins stormed out of the house. As he drove away, he worried a change might be taking place at Madam Honey's house. He just could not understand why a bunch of whores and a faggot would be so concerned about the death of a fatherless child.

Watching him spin the tires on his patrol car as he left Madam Honey's, Mary thought, *'I know Sheriff Jenkins don't think any of us as human. He don't think of us at all unless we is providin' him with one of two pleasures—money or sex.'*

Mary smiled to herself as the Sheriff's car left in a cloud of dust. It had given her great pleasure to have heard the anger Madam Honey had caused him.

26

Cherry (Heather Lee Witman)

We used to live in that house," Cherry said, pointing to an old brown shack situated behind a brick house located in a well-to-do neighborhood. "This was where all the rich people lived before they started building houses on the other side of town. My momma used to clean for the lady who lived in the house up front. Momma said she was cleaning for the lady a long time before I was born. I never told anybody this, but my daddy is the man who was married to the lady my momma cleaned for. Momma said the lady suspected her husband of messin' around with her and even asked Momma. But my momma lied to her and said she would never do such a thing to the lady. When I was born with red hair, the lie was made known. I got a half-sister that looks just like me. Momma said we take after our father. I don't recall my daddy's name. I guess his name don't matter today. Momma said he was a big man with a mane of fiery red hair."

Chocolate had no idea why Cherry was revealing all this to her. She had been under the impression they would be taking a walk to the bar. Had she known she was going to invite her into her past, Chocolate was sure she would have declined.

"They moved awhile ago, when I was younger. I don't recall Momma ever saying it was on account of me, but I know I had a lot to do with it. I'm sure the woman couldn't take a little nigga girl livin' in the same town as her daughter. Momma said it was people who chased the woman off. Every now and again some stranger, who didn't know any better, would ask the woman if she had another daughter. The woman's mouth would get tight around the edges and she'd tell the stranger, "No!"

Momma never actually saw this happen, but it got back to her plenty of times. I just made up the story 'bout not knowin' who my daddy is. Saying I don't know makes it easier for me. For some reason it seems to take some of the shame away."

"You ever see your father?" Chocolate asked.

"No. He left when his wife moved out of town. I suppose he loved his wife. My momma was simply doing her duty, like I do mine. Only difference is, I get paid for my pleasures."

Chocolate wanted to turn around and leave. She did not like the emotions all this information gave her. She did not like to see Cherry being hurt about a part of her past she had stored away. But what puzzled Chocolate was why Cherry had chosen her as the person to whom she revealed her past. Asking if she could leave would have been rude and hurt Cherry's feelings. Therefore, she decided to stand firm in spite of the discomfort Cherry's disclosure brought her. If Cherry could live through it and remain sane, then she certainly could listen and keep her sanity.

"I tried to understand why she left me. I reasoned that I was a burden worth relieving. In my mind it was a fair exchange. The older I got, I realized how hard it is to live this life we are handed. With me out of the way, I figured my momma could finally get a chance to live. I'm grown, I told myself, and all she'd done is in the past. If I want anything better, I gotta do for myself. I cain't blame her anymore. Then, just that simple, I went from hating my momma to forgiving her. I made up my mind to forget all the bad and I remembered all the good. Ya see, it wasn't all that bad. My momma worked hard, but she loved hard. True, she worked harder than she loved. But that's 'cause she had to work in order to take care of me.

"Chocolate, we both know life isn't easy for a single, colored woman. No matter what you all think, life don't give a damn about me being a light-skinned nigga. My momma would drag me around while she cleaned houses and sneak me chocolates and all kind of candies. It was all she could do to try and make my life a little better."

Cherry continued, "After witnessing life and death in the same day, I don't know how my momma could have left me. Oh, when I held that baby, I loved it stronger than I have ever loved. That baby girl wasn't even mine and I loved her. I didn't realize how much I loved her until she was gone. I know she was never here, but, at the same time, she was. As I watched her, I imagined her crawling around with that pretty polish on her hands and feet. My mind even heard her calling out her first word, 'Momma.' I know the word wouldn't have been for me, but it could have. After falling in love with somebody else's child, I can only wonder why my momma up and left me for a whore to raise. Why, Chocolate? Why?"

This was a hard one and Chocolate thought a moment before saying, "We don't all get the mommas we think we deserve. Some of us don't even get a momma, period. Take me for instance. Mine died before my mind could form a memory of her."

"That's just it. She died. She didn't up and leave you." Cherry answered, her eyes big with surprise.

"Cherry, I don't have the answers to none of the questions that are on your mind. All I know is what I experienced. My past is far from a bed of roses. I say we leave here and head on back to the house."

"All right." Cherry turned and followed Chocolate's lead.

27

Madam Honey (Abigail Richard)

This boy sho' is big! Look at all this hair," Madam Honey lightly rubbed her hand through the baby's hair, careful not to put pressure on his soft spot. She was sitting on the couch in the living room holding the child on her lap. Madam Honey had fallen in love with the baby and did not try to conceal the fact that she had taken to him— even though the child's presence made her nights shorter and her days longer.

There never seemed enough time in the day for her to sit and just love on the baby. So, instead of hanging around the night crowd that gathered at her home, she left Toni in charge of things and went up to bed. She wanted to be up in time to witness Delroy open his eyes. The baby's schedule had not changed since he entered the world. He was up at five in the morning. He would wake up, do a little crying, eat and fall right back into his slumber.

Madam Honey still was not permitted to go near the child in his mother's presence. The girl took to hissing whenever Madam Honey entered the room. It was not until around nine in the morning that she would have her chance. At that time, Madam Honey would send Mary into the room to get Delroy. From nine until he was ready to be breastfed was how long Madam Honey was allowed to care for the baby boy. She took great care in everything she did concerning the child.

Since the mother did not speak, Delroy was the name Madam Honey had chosen for the child the moment she had laid eyes on him. It was her brother's name—her twin brother who had died of malnutrition at the age of two. Madam Honey did not recall much about her brother. Basically, all she knew was what her grandmother had told her as she grew up. Her grandmother always maintained that, had she knew how things were, she would have come and gotten the both of them. By the time she had received word of the situation, it was too late.

Interrupting her own train of thought and keeping her eyes on the baby, Madam Honey asked Mary, "You think she gonna be upset 'bout me callin' the boy Delroy? He's a lot bigger than the girl was, but they look just alike. You think she ever gonna tell us what she wants us to call him? He needs a name. All babies need a name. What you think about Delroy? He reminds me of my brother. I'll call him Delroy until she says different."

"*You* gonna give her baby a name?" Mary asked. "I think that's kinda strange. I mean, it ain't normal for a woman to name another woman's child. You might want to give it a little time before you take to namin' the boy. She may have it different in her mind. I watch as she smiles and interacts with him some. I'm thinkin' she has plans on talkin' sometime soon. Seems to me there is somethin' stoppin' her voice. I can tell she wants to say somethin' to him."

"Well, we cain't do him like we did the girl. It ain't normal to refer to him as the baby. It was all right with the girl. The girl was put in the ground. She didn't have enough time to be named. That and the fact that that preacher didn't care nothin' 'bout the baby he was layin' to rest. All he worried 'bout was the twenty-five dollars he was paid to preach that sorry-ass sermon."

"Well," Mary continued, "we couldn't find a preacher in town who would step foot on your property."

"Correction," Madam Honey stated. "We couldn't find a preacher who would step foot on my property in the daylight."

"I stand corrected," Mary said with a grin.

Mary watched as Madam Honey cooed and tickled the baby under his chin. She listened as she sang jingles and lullabies in the child's ear. Before this moment, Mary had never seen the woman so blissful. She had seen her happy with greed, but never happy with life. For some reason, the sight of the older woman's satisfaction scared Mary. In her heart she understood that the child could be taken away from Madam Honey and never be replaced. If and when that happened, Mary knew his absence would bring a depression that would leave Madam Honey in a black hole.

"Have Toni bring me that bag that's on my bed. I sent for him a new toy. It's a bear that sings the alphabet. I know he's got awhile to go before he'll be able to talk, let alone sing. I still think he gonna enjoy listenin' to it."

"Okay," Mary said, leaving the living room to retrieve the bear.

28
Mary Ann Tobert (Bit-of-Honey)

ary sat on the front porch and watched as the rain fell from the sunny sky. It had come down hard and heavy, with no warning. One minute, Toni and Marcus had been working the land. The next thing Mary knew, they were both running for cover. As they ran, Mary had to look twice to make sure she was not seeing things. Toni's hat had blown off, giving Mary a full view of the soft reddish hair that covered her scalp. It was about five inches long. Before the hat had been blown off, Mary had been under the impression Toni was still bald. Silently, Mary watched as Toni chased the errant hat a good distance across the field before she caught up with it.

"Can I sit on the porch until it stops raining?" Marcus asked as he stood shivering in the rain.

"I suppose so," Mary replied.

"How long you think the rain is gonna come down like this? I hope not long. It's a bad sign, rain coming down while the sun is still shining. You know what it means, don't you?" Marcus answered his question before Mary could reply. "It means the devil is fighting his wife. By the looks of all this rain, he's beating her pretty good."

"I always heard that rain coming while the sun is shining meant that God was having a good cry," Toni chimed in.

"That don't make sense," Marcus said, looking at Toni as if she had lost her mind. "Why would God cry?"

"There's lots God could cry about," Toni said, entering the conversation. "Look at how crazy this world is. You don't think the way people living is enough to make God cry? Take you, for instance. Until I had the privilege to work on the side of you, I thought you was just a simple-minded fool. After working with you in that field, I got a chance to know the kind of person you is. All you want out of life is to make your aunt happy and find you a nice woman to care for. Think of all the people who passed you by. Most think about you like I used to. Not many will have the pleasure of meeting the real Marcus; the Marcus who is careful not to kill a garden snake when he is working the field. Not many people think a snake is important enough to save. Now, if that ain't enough to make God cry, I don't know what is. God created the snake just as he created you and me."

Marcus sat dumbfounded as he listened to Toni's statement. He knew exactly what she was referring to. He knew that when he spoke, sometimes he sounded like a child. He also knew even children understood what they wanted out of life. Most times when he held a conversation with an adult, they paid no attention to what was coming out of his mouth. Still, he was expected to take all what they said to heart. Adults often made him nervous and was why he often got confused. His mind was not the problem. It was the treatment he received that threw him off balance. Working at Madam Honey's, he found that conversation came easy. The only time he was yelled at was when Madam Honey came around. When he dealt with the younger women, he could relax and respond in a comprehensible manner.

"I'm gonna go in the house and get you some dinner to take home with you. The way things look, we won't be working for a few days. Even if the rain slows down some, we gonna have to wait a few days before we can get back out there. It's gonna be too wet, too much mud," Toni announced.

"She's right 'bout that," Mary interjected. "The rain is gonna give you a good break. You all been workin' so hard. I'm pretty sure you need it."

Toni returned to the porch with more food than Marcus had ever seen at one time. His eyes almost fell out of his head as he stared at the food that was overflowing from the basket. Inside were eight pieces of fried chicken, half of a meatloaf, and smothered pork chops. Besides the meat, there were five nice-sized baked potatoes, four ears of corn, and a bushel of greens. That was not all. On top of the wrapped food, Toni had placed two loaves of bread and, cradled in a separate paper bag located under her armpit, eight freshly ripe peaches.

"Take this," Toni said, handing Marcus some money. "And buy some butter. This should hold you and your aunt over until the ground is dry enough for us to work again."

With his good hand, Marcus stuffed all the food together in the basket. "Thank you, Toni. My aunt sho' is gonna be glad to see all this food."

"I almost forgot." Toni went in the house and came back out with a jar of homemade blackberry jam. "This jam will taste real good on that bread. Don't eat all those peaches fresh. Fry some. Smother them in brown sugar and deep fry 'em. The heat will turn the sugar into a thick glaze."

"I sure will," Marcus lied. He knew his aunt didn't have the sugar to put on the peaches nor did she have the fresh lard in which to fry them. All the lard at their house was very old.

Both women silently watched as Marcus took the food and ran through the rain.

"That was nice of you," Mary said to Toni after he had disappeared.

"He deserves it. That Marcus is a hard worker."

"You work pretty hard yourself. I don't know how you do it, but you do a good job," Mary complimented.

"What I do is what any woman can do if she puts her mind to it. Think about it. Slave women had to do just as much as slave men. I know today things are different but, if you think about it, I ain't doin' nothing that hasn't been done before my time."

"You gonna let your hair grow out?" Mary asked the question before she could stop herself. "It looks good on you. I mean, what little I saw. You was quite a distance but, from what I saw, you look good."

"Thanks," Toni said, taking her hat off and running her fingers through her hair. "I been thinking 'bout it. One day, I'm thinkin' I'm gonna grow it out and the next day, I feel like cuttin' it bald again. Right now, I'm between thoughts. The only thing I'm sure 'bout is the fact that I want to do somethin' different."

After a pause, Mary said, "I can do it for you. I bet if I were to straighten it out, it would be at least two more inches in length. It's all curled up now 'cause you got a good grade of hair. It wouldn't take much heat to straighten it out. It looks thick, too. Yea, you'd look real good with some curls all over your head."

"I'll keep that in mind."

"Madam Honey wants to know if you gonna make a banana puddin' tonight," Chocolate said as she opened the door, interrupting the conversation between Mary and Toni.

"Yeah," Toni replied, quickly putting her hat back on her head.

Mary waited until Chocolate had gone back into the house before she spoke again. "It will get better."

Toni did not say a word, but continued staring off into the sunny rain-filled sky.

"I know how bad you feel. To be honest, I don't know how you able to remain in this house," Mary commented.

"Where else can I go? I'm forced to be here. I'm not like Pretty. I don't have men waiting at my feet. Look at me, Mary. What other choice do I have? I'm not here 'cause I want to be. I'm here 'cause the world don't want me. This is the only place I can be me."

Toni let out a short huff. "Ha. Now that's a good reason for God to spill tears. One of His creations findin' adjustment in a whorehouse. What you think He think 'bout me findin' refuge in a whorehouse? Naw. I'm forced to stay here in pain."

Mary responded, "You have to be stronger than the situation. I know it's hard, but let it go and move on. I know it's easier said than done. But, I also know it's possible. I was in your predicament before. That's what led me to Madam Honey. My lover abandoned me; somethin' similar to what happened to you. He didn't leave me for money, a good time, not even another woman. He did just like Pretty. He left 'cause he could. I blamed myself for a long time."

"How did you stop blaming yourself?"

"Got tired. I simply got tired of lookin' for what I did wrong. Lookin' for mistakes I made; mistakes that didn't exist. Before comin' here, I questioned everything 'bout me. Hell, I even had nerve to put the reason he left on my momma and she had no idea he left me. I was in a state of disorder and severe agony. That's the condition I had myself in. I was a poor mess before walkin' up these steps."

Mary pointed toward the front of the house as she continued, "My lover was the only man I had taken to my bed. I left home thinking he would be the only man ever in my bed. Survival and confusion is what led me here."

"But I love her," Toni said in a low, tremulous voice.

"That's the saddest part of all our stories," Mary continued. "I still love him, but love don't turn on and off like a water faucet. I tried hatin' him, but it drained me. It took too much energy to pretend I didn't want him in my life. I wanted it— still do at times. I guess it's like he's become a part of me, like air. The battle is never over. One thing I can take pride in is the fact that I'm winnin' the battle. I don't waste time on wantin', hatin' or needin'. I'm focusin' more on myself. I'm tryin' to find my own comfort zone in life. Whenever a cravin' for him comes across my mind, I look at it as a good time that I was fortunate enough to experience.

"There are many who will never experience what Chocolate gave you or what Travis gave me. Know in your heart that of all the people they take to their beds, not many of them get to know the person you were introduced to. Most times they sleep with the individuals and keep steppin'. I often wonder what was it about me that made him want to place his shoes under my mattress and try and make a life.

"I gotta believe he had good intentions 'cause he asked me to come with him and I went. He didn't have to take me along. I gave him everything. There was no more for me to do for him or to him. I figure he took me 'cause, at that time in his life, he loved me. The decision he made concernin' leavin' me, I have decided to chalk it up that he was just bein' a man. I also reasoned that if he hadn't taken me along with him, my heart would have been broken anyway.

You gotta come up with your reason, Toni. Just know that what the both of you shared was special, but it wasn't meant to last. Enjoy the memory of what you had and let the rest go."

Toni was silent for a few moments before she replied, "I never looked at it in those terms. It's just that I was bankin' on us puttin' in life together. I wanted us to grow old together."

Toni got up and walked toward the front door. As she opened it, she turned and with a little smile, looked Mary in the eyes and said, "Thank you."

29
The Silent Girl

Silently, she watched as Mary handled the baby.
'*It is my baby,*' she had to keep reminding herself. '*One is missing...a girl. I gave birth to two babies. Where had they put the baby girl?*

'*I remember all the strange women crowding around me when the babies were born. I recall them screaming with joy that two babies were born, a boy and a girl. But I don't remember two babies crying. All I heard was the cry of one baby. After that, I don't remember much as I spent most of my time sleeping. It seemed that no matter how hard I tried to fight off the sleep, it overtook my body. I remember sometimes waking up and one baby was suckling my breast.*'

Fatigue had prevented her from asking the whereabouts of the other baby. She reasoned it was the walk that had made her so slumberous. It had taken all the energy she had. When she had gotten word her husband had been shot and killed in a whorehouse two towns over, she had walked the entire way. During the whole route she had felt the babies fighting in her stomach. It was as if they had been battling for space and nourishment. She knew her babies had wanted her to rest. They had wanted her to furnish what they needed in order to be born healthy. But stopping had not been an option.

What drove her on was that she wanted to face the woman who had stolen her life—snatched away the protection she and her babies needed. She had ignored the babies kicking and crying for nourishment, especially water. They were not going to detour her from arriving at the evil house tucked away in the forest. Her emotions were so overpowering that she forgot about food and water. When she had no energy, she drank from streams and lakes as she passed them. She even took to soaking the bottom of her skirt and sucking the water out of it when the babies begged for something to drink. When they cramped her stomach too bad, she ate dandelions, wild berries, and tree bark. A couple of times she took to eating ants and snails. She remembered her daddy telling her that they had protein. Her only concern had been to meet up with the woman who had stolen her husband—stolen the good life that had been hers.

Once she had found the house, she had been so tired and delirious that she could not speak. All she could remember was falling and waking up fighting. In fact, she barely remembered giving birth. Then, after the babies had been born, she slept—a very deep sleep. It was the food that had originally calmed her down. The one called Mary had brought her everything she could eat, but is seemed she had never stopped being thirsty. The sugar milk Mary brought had helped some, but it did not take the dry feeling that seemed to be stuck in her throat.

When she had first arrived at the house, her voice had been completely gone. It seemed every time she had tried to verbalize how she felt about the death of her husband, no sound would come out. She could not recall when she had lost her voice. She only remembered talking to herself on her way to the whorehouse. Most of the time she had talked to her babies, instructing them to be still. For some reason, she had not concerned herself with them; their daddy needed her. Their daddy needed her to go to the woman's house who had taken his life and bring her down. Her goal was to break the woman; break the woman who had put fear in the hearts of all the colored men and women four counties over.

Lying in the bed, she tried to recall if she had managed to hum before the babies were born or if it was a dream. She chalked the memory up as a dream and turned her worries to her baby girl.

"You up?" Mary said entering the room.

The young mute girl looked at Mary's wide-eyed smile and wondered if she knew where her baby girl was. She liked Mary. It seemed as if she would be considered decent, if she was not living in a whorehouse. Plus, Mary had been taking to her, telling her a lot of things about Madam Honey. Most she could not recall, but she did gather that Mary did not think too highly of the obese woman.

"You sho' have been sleepin' a lot. It'd be nice if you stepped outside of this room and got yourself some fresh air. It's nice and cool outside. You just missed a pretty rain. The other day it was rainin' while the sun was still shinin' as bright as could be."

Mary went over and sat on the edge of the bed. "I know you ain't much on talkin'. At the same time, I feel your pain. I know you understand what I'm sayin'. So if you could just nod your head yes or no when I speak, I wouldn't feel so foolish."

The girl simply looked at Mary with the same non-expression she had since she had arrived. Even though she favored Mary a little more than the other girls, she did not think of her as a friend.

"If you ain't ready to speak, I understand. You been through a lot. I know how it feels to lose a baby. It hurts real bad."

Upon hearing this, tears welled up in the girl's eyes. *My baby is dead. That's why I didn't hear a second cry. Now my baby and my husband are gone,'* she thought.

30

Madam Honey (Abigail Richard)

Madam Honey sat quietly as she handed Sheriff Jenkins his money. He looked at the thin stack of bills and frowned. Without counting it, he knew it was short. Before he could say anything, she told him, "Business is slow. It'll pick up soon enough and things will be runnin' smooth again."

"Seems to me things would be a lot better if you got rid of that ugly ass mute girl and her baby. You turnin' these whores into wet nurses. That new girl, Mary, or Bit-of-Honey is spendin' more time tendin' to that baby than she is the men. I won't stand for this. Somethin' is gonna have to give. I don't know if the mayor will be able to protect you with you payin' him like this." Sheriff Jenkins pushed the money in Madam Honey's face and continued, "I don't know what's gotten into you. I thought you was smarter than the rest of the nigga women I deal with. Seems what you doin' is provin' to be just as dumb. I'm not gonna instruct you on how to fix the problem. I am gonna tell you that it needs to be fixed."

As Sheriff Jerkins walked to the door, he said over his shoulder, "Best you have the ladies put in some overtime; like work on a Sunday or somethin'. I expect the difference to paid the next time I visit." He then calmly exited the house.

Madam Honey sat in a rage. She said to herself, '*I hate that white man for insultin' me in my own house. I hate the way he forcing me to run my business as he sees fit.*'

For years Sheriff Jenkins had been trying to get Madam Honey to open her doors on Sundays. It was not that she claimed to be a woman of the Lord, but Sunday was the day she gave her girls off. Even slaves were permitted to have a day of rest. How did he expect the girls to do a good job if they never had time to themselves? She used to be a whore herself. She knew how hard the work was.

Since the silent girl had arrived, Madam Honey had noticed Sheriff Jenkins snooping around more than usual. She knew he disapproved of the girl and baby staying at the house. Also, she knew he would not bring up his dissatisfaction until it affected him personally. His money coming up short affected him. To Madam Honey's way of thinking, she had been paying that man more than his share of money for over twenty years.

All these years, not once had she been late or short. Not once had she tried to slick him out of a dime. Now, the one time she came up a little short, he all but spit in her face and disrespected her. Also, he had called her a nigga and had said it as if he meant it. Madam Honey reasoned that the reason he had used that tone was because that was really how he felt about her.

Sheriff Jenkins cared for her just as much as he cared for the baby boy with whom she had fallen in love with. She had taken such a liking to the child that she named the boy after her dead brother. Without any thought or care, Sheriff Jenkins had instructed her to get rid of what she dearly loved—throw Delroy and his mother out of her life.

Madam Honey did not know how to stand up to Sheriff Jenkins. In fact, she did not know how to stand up to any white man. All she had been allowed to do was what he allowed her to do. He had made it clear from the beginning that if she was not going to fund him with money, then she could go straight to hell. He had given her permission to kill any black man who entered her home and disrespected her. But if a white man did the same thing, she was to send for him to handle the problem.

Still sitting in the chair, she closed her eyes and saw herself for what she really was—a modern day slave. The only difference between her and a field hand was that she got to keep some of the money; that and the fact she ran her plantation most of the time. Her master, Sheriff Jenkins, simply came through and picked up the money.

Madam Honey's main thought was how to make the Sheriff understand that she needed that baby boy in her home. In her mind, she went over ways she could explain it to him so that he would realize that his money would be right even if the child was there. She told herself that she would lie and say the baby was sick and that was the reason Mary was tending to him. It was so important to Madam Honey that she decided she would dip into her personal savings in order to give the Sheriff the money she owed him. She figured that as long as his money was right, he would not try and make her put Delroy and his mother out on the streets.

"He left pretty upset," Chocolate said, walking into the room with Madam Honey.

"Yea, I been slacking up on you girls. I won't put all the blame on you all. Things is gonna get back to the way they were. Money has to be made. If I cain't pay for protection, we won't be protected. That girl is gonna have to start tending to her own baby at night. Either that or she's gonna have to go."

The last thing she wanted was for Chocolate to know that she was losing control of the situation. She wanted all the girls to think she was the mistress of her own home.

Madam Honey was quiet for a moment and then she stated, "I don't want her to leave. I enjoy havin' Delroy around, but it's up to her to do more with her baby. I like the little fella. He does somethin' for me."

Chocolate replied, "He does somethin' for everybody. I know everybody will work real hard to keep him here. His momma seems to be doin' a lot better. She ain't speakin' or nothin' but she don't sleep all the time. I think it will be all right to leave him with her through the night. Mary would die if Sheriff Jenkins put them out. It wouldn't shock me if she left with them."

"It wouldn't shock me either."

31

Cherry (Heather Lee Witman)

Cherry had gotten up extra early so she could spend time alone with Delroy. Before getting the baby, she went into the kitchen and made herself a glass of orange juice. Madam Honey had made it clear to her that she could not handle the baby if she had been drinking.

Taking the baby out onto the front porch, Cherry sat pretending not to notice Marcus eying her as she held Delroy in her arms. It had been two weeks since Marcus had returned to work. The ground had finally dried enough for him to start working again.

Marcus worked long hours. To Cherry, it seemed as if he worked so he would not have to go home. It was not a secret how he felt about his aunt. She reasoned he loved the woman only because he had no other choice. He did not know any other type of love. All the beatings and being talked down to was all he knew. Sometimes Cherry had seen the difference in the treatment Madam Honey gave him. She would try to send him home, but he refused. It had gotten to the point where he just hung around the house looking for something to do. If Madam Honey said anything, Marcus would always remind her that all the extra work he did was free of charge.

Cherry could not figure out if not having to pay him or the change of heart Delroy had brought about that allowed Madam Honey to let him stay.

Madam Honey had changed a lot since the mute girl had arrived. Once the babies had been born, things had only gotten better. True, when Sheriff Jenkins had come around and complained about the mute girl, she had taken a little more of their money. One night she had taken all their earnings. She had explained that taking the money was the only way she could stay in business under her own terms. No one complained. Everybody knew her own terms meant Sheriff Jenkins allowing Delroy and his mother to stay.

Since Mary had been instructed she could no longer be up at night with Delroy, before she went to work, she made sure the mute girl and the baby had everything they needed. She placed plates of food, water, and plenty of clothes in the room before she went downstairs to entertain the men. In fact, she had been given a different room in which to turn her tricks. If that plan did not work out, Madam Honey had plans to send the mute girl and the baby into Lacey's room. If the baby got sick, she expected Lacey to step in and perform the fatherly duties.

Sheriff Jenkins did not deal with Lacey at all because just the sight of Lacey made him nervous. He did not talk down to him like he did everyone else in the house either. Instead, the Sheriff acted as if Lacey did not exist. Once, he told Madam Honey that something about a man sleeping with another man was not natural. With the Sheriff's way of thinking, he was a waste of space. Sometimes he mentioned that he did not think Lacey brought much money into the house. She kept Lacey's clients a secret from the Sheriff.

"Can I hold the baby?" Marcus asked, walking toward Cherry. His question had interrupted her quiet reverie.

"You too dirty. You cain't hold no baby with all that mud caked up on you," she snapped.

"What if I go around back and hose myself down? Then can I hold him?" he insisted.

Cherry took one look in Marcus's eyes and knew he wanted nothing more at that moment than to have Delroy in his arms. She understood so said, "Hurry. I don't want Madam Honey to see you and get mad at me."

Marcus left and returned with his body and clothes all soaking wet but clean.

"Here. Sit down so you won't drop him. He's so small, a fall could do him some serious harm," Cherry explained.

Marcus sat on the porch and readied himself to handle the child. "How old is he?"

"'Bout a month and a half. He ain't been here long, but he's growin' like a weed."

"I ain't never held a baby before." Marcus was tender with the child. His rigid body informed Cherry that he was nervous. "I see the women at the church holding babies all the time. I always wanted to hold one, but whenever I was around one, Aunt Dorothy hurried me away. Linda Stone had herself a baby girl. She is cute. I think she's about a month old. I knew better than to ask to hold her. It would have been an excuse for a beating once I got home. It's been like that since I was a little boy, people sending me away when I step near a baby."

"They don't mean no harm," Cherry said. "People is real protective of their babies."

"He's perfect." Marcus took his good hand and counted the baby's fingers. "I wasn't lucky enough to be born perfect."

"Nobody is perfect," Cherry said. "We all have defects. You was born the way God intended you to be born. Don't start talkin' silly, Marcus, or I'll take the baby away from you."

"I'm sorry. I won't say anything silly. I just want to hold him for awhile. He's so soft and he smells good. He smells better than flowers."

"That's all the powder and baby soap we use to clean him," she explained.

"Ain't that somethin'? Babies got they own soap. I never knew that. I was in the mind of thinkin' they used the same soap as us."

"Naw," Cherry said laughing. "They use they own. It's a special soap that's made for their delicate skin. Babies are different than grown people. Take the soft spot that's in the middle of their heads. It has to be protected until it gets hard, like everybody else's."

"I didn't know nothin' 'bout a spot in the top of babies' heads."

"Well, you had one, too, when you was born," she explained.

Marcus took his nub and rubbed the top of his head. "How is his momma holdin' up? I seen her when she arrived, but I ain't seen her since. How she doin'? I figure she gotta be somewhere in the house. Ain't nobody in town talkin' 'bout a new whore workin' at Madam Honey's so I figure she ain't a whore. I even done had some men approach me 'bout the baby's momma. They be asking me if I've seen her. They know the baby don't belong to none of you regular girls. They say they can sometimes hear a baby crying."

Cherry thought real hard before answering Marcus's question. It was the look in his eyes that helped her decide to tell him the truth. He looked genuinely concerned for the child. "His momma hasn't been feelin' well since she arrived. She's still sick and aint well, but is gettin' better. We all pitchin' in and helpin' out until she can get her health back."

"Well, I hope she gets herself together 'cause he gonna want his momma. I'm a grown man and there are days I still wish for mine. My aunt is nice enough and I know she means me well, but I sure would like to know what it feels like to have a real momma. Somebody to love me 'cause they want to and not 'cause they keepin' a promise they made on a deathbed."

"It felt fine,"Cherry said before she knew it.

"Yo' momma did up and leave you one day. I'm sorry. Least you had one for a short while. You think his momma gonna be able to tend to him?"

"I don't know."

Personally, Cherry was hoping Delroy would be able to stay with them forever. "If his momma don't come around, he'll be fine. Who else you know got five women lookin' after them? Lacey may as well be a woman."

"I guess you got a point," he answered.

Just then, Cherry heard Madam Honey's heavy footsteps headed their way. She whispered, "Give him here. Madam Honey is comin'!"

Marcus quickly handed the baby to her as he said, "I better get back to work. She gonna be madder than a wet cat if she see me sittin' around."

He then turned and rushed back to the field.

32

The Silent Girl

How long I been lying here?" the silent girl asked, startling Mary. "And where's my baby girl?"

Her voice startled Mary so, she dropped the glass of sweet milk she was carrying and it shattered into pieces on the floor, cutting her foot.

"You can talk?" Mary said, ignoring the blood coming from her foot.

"Where is she?" The sound of the girl's voice was weak and raspy, carrying a tone of seriousness and anger.

"You been down quite awhile. I was beginnin' to think you was gonna miss your son's first steps. He's crawlin' and gettin' around pretty good." Mary bent down and examined her bloody foot. The cut was not too deep, but she would need to clean it up.

"She's gone over to the other side," Mary said, referring to the baby girl. "You don't remember? Madam Honey had a nice home-going for her. You were there. She made me drag you out of bed and Lacey put you in a chair. You didn't wanna go, but I pleaded with you. I thought you understood when I explained it was for your dead baby. I guess you were sleepwalking. She was born with no life in her."

"Oh. I thought I dreamed that." The girl was quiet for a moment then said, "I can vaguely recall a funeral. I don't remember seeing my baby. I don't even recall holding her. Did I hold her?"

"Yes," Mary lied. She was too afraid to tell the girl she had never fully opened her eyes after the children had been born. As it was, they had carried her to the gravesite and, even then, she had sat in a chair silently crying with her eyes closed.

"Good. I don't want my baby to pass on to the other side and not have her own momma's hands touch her."

"No, it wasn't a dream." Mary did not know how to reply to the last part of the girl's statement. "Maybe it's better you don't recall. 'cause you got Delroy and he's a special child."

"Delroy? Who is Delroy?" the girl asked in a surprised tone. "I don't know a Delroy."

"Delroy is your baby boy."

"My baby boy is to be called Richard. He is to be named after his dead father."

Mary stood quietly, not knowing how to explain the child's name so she quickly left the room and returned with her foot wrapped in a piece of white cloth. "You ready to take a real bath and a walk?" she asked brightly. "I been wipin' you down in the bed in order to keep you clean. I also took to turning you so you wouldn't develop bedsores."

"Yea, I need to get myself together so I can get back home. I know my people is worried about me."

"I hope you don't plan on leaving until you fully well. You came here in bad condition. You was fighting like a deranged woman."

"I don't remember," the girl lied.

"What's your name? We been calling you the silent girl or Delroy's momma."

"Annie Mae. Annie Mae is all you need to know."

"Well, Annie Mae, it's high time I took you to the bathroom and introduced you to our tub. Madam Honey got three bathrooms in this house. I bet you ain't never heard of such a thing in your life. I thought it was strange when I first saw all three of them. They come in handy with us being whores and all."

"Would you please bring me Richard so I can bathe him with me?" "He's gone. Toni and Chocolate took him into town. They'll be back soon. They took him to get fitted for some clothes by Martha, the woman in town who makes our clothes. Madam Honey is having them made for him. Martha broke her leg. She couldn't get around to coming out here, so Madam Honey sent him to her."

"If her leg is broke, how she gonna work?"

"I said her leg was broke. I didn't say nothin' 'bout her hands. They'll be back soon enough. In a few hours it'll be time for Chocolate to work. Martha is taking measurements and then they'll be headed back this way."

"Why you all doin' so much for me and my baby? Havin' clothes made and tendin' to me like I'm part of your family?"

"What's so special about givin' a baby clothes? That boy grows so fast we really don't have much of a choice. What? You want him runnin' around here naked? And you bein' his momma, you should be glad that he got somebody lookin' after him. Was we supposed to let you die? We ain't doing too much of nothin'. We was simply helpin' the both of you out," Mary explained.

Annie Mae lay in the tub, trying to make her mind remember what had taken place that had led her to this house. Then she remembered it all—it was a woman named Madam Honey who had shot her husband. She remembered the grown men back home shaking their heads and wiping away tears over something they knew could not be revenged. It was the protection of a white man that prevented Madam Honey from facing any judicial procedures when it came to killing any black man, even if the man was killed for nothing.

Everybody within hearing distance knew the boy had only been playing around when he had insulted the enormous woman. They all knew he had not meant any harm by the comment he made. He had simply been talking trash— something colored folks do all the time. But the man Madam Honey had killed this time was not any "no count nigga." He was a hard-working man who had a new family to care for.

The man was truly a boy in age. He was only beginning to prove himself a man. His marrying so young was proof enough. Did he not take a young girl's hand in marriage when he found out she was carrying his children, and two of them? He did not run off and pretend he never bedded the girl. Now, he was dead and someone was going to be made to pay for his death.

Annie Mae soaked in the tub and wondered, '*Why did my husband have to frequent a place like this—a place full of nasty women? This is a place where the women are so vile that the house needs three bathrooms. He had been raised better. At least I thought he had been raised better. Was his manhood so out of control that the lusting for pleasure led him to such a corrupt place?*'

She had no time to be upset with the decision her husband had made to enter Madam Honey's house. All her feelings were bottled up in anger that was directed toward the woman who had killed him.

"Who took to calling Richard Delroy?" Annie Mae asked Mary, interrupting her thoughts.

"Madam Honey. She named him after her twin brother. He died when he was two."

"Well, my baby ain't gonna be called no Delroy. He's gonna be called Richard, after his own dead daddy."

"I'm sorry to hear his daddy is dead," Mary whispered.

Annie Mae simply stared at Mary for a few moments the said, "Do you mind me asking how he died?"

"Yes, I do."

33

Toni (Rainie Holloway)

S it still!" Chocolate snapped at Toni as she parted and tussled with her hair. "You gonna look real pretty with these waves on your head. I'm glad you let your hair grow out and stopped dressing so manly. You looked good the other way, but you look much better like this."

Chocolate stood back and admired the new look she had created. "Yea, you is real pretty. You look just as good as Pretty. You got a natural beauty about yourself, too. It's always been there. I never understood why you hid it. You keeping your head bald and wearing men's clothes; all that stuff still doesn't hinder people from seeing how beautiful you are."

"How long my hair gonna stay like this?" Toni asked, staring at her reflection in the mirror. Actually, she liked the look. It surprised her that she liked looking like a woman. The new hairstyle made her feel like a real woman. She felt both gorgeous and odd at the same time, questioning the image that she was staring at. What surprised her most was that she had not thought it was possible to look like a woman and feel good about it. The only other time she had fixed herself up, she had been punished for it. This time, things were different. Toni felt pretty and was told she was pretty by the only person who had ever shown her any affection. She stood and thoroughly examined the new person reflected in the mirror.

"I *am* pretty," she said out loud. At that very moment, Toni decided to accept everything Madam Honey had told her the morning she spoke about the pain Chocolate had caused in her world.

"What do you mean?" Chocolate could sense the confusion in Toni's voice. "You are one of most beautiful people I have ever met. Your beauty is both inside and out. You are carin', you listen, and, on top of all that, you look good while you do it. I wish you could see all that I see. Sometimes you come across as if your eyes don't work. I never understood that 'bout you. I never understood why you allow people to walk all over you.

"Toni, you don't have to hide in this house and let the world outside pass you by. You need to start makin' yourself up and steppin' in the sunshine. You'll die if you continue livin' like you don't need what's outside of this place.

"I'm scared of rejection. I'm scared if I wander too far off the porch that I'll make a mistake. Then, if I make a mistake, people will blame me for it."

Chocolate let out a small laugh. "Child, please. Folks are born to make mistakes. Think about it. Jesus was born for just that purpose. I don't claim to know much about the Bible, but I do know this: Jesus was put here so folks could accuse him of doin' wrong and kill him for nothin'. Now, if that ain't the biggest mistake of all, I don't know what it is. Toni, answer me this."

She turned around and looked into Chocolate's eyes for the first time since she had entered her room. "How you expect to learn anything if you stunt yourself 'cause that's just what you doin' by hidin' out in this house. What you gonna do if somethin' happens to Madam Honey? Where you gonna go? How you gonna take care of yourself?

"You need to learn to be independent. You cain't expect Madam

Honey to be here for you until the end of time. You only some good to her as long as you have a purpose in *her* life. We both know that means as long as you can provide her with money."

"How do I grow?" Toni whispered. "How do I move on? I ain't never been strong enough to do anything by myself."

"You just do it. Ain't no instructions on how you go 'bout doin' it. It's more like an instinct. It's somethin' God put in everything He created. You need to know He didn't forget about you."

After Chocolate left her room, Toni, still somewhat dazed, surprised and puzzled, mentally went over the recent events and conversation that had happened. She still was not sure why she had allowed Chocolate into her bedroom. It was early in the morning when Chocolate had knocked on her door. The last john had left the house and Toni was getting settled in her room after cleaning the kitchen.

"You up?" Chocolate had asked as she lightly tapped on Toni's bedroom door. Hearing her voice, Toni had wanted to lie and pretend she had not heard her knocking. It was something in the sound of Chocolate's voice that had made her get out of bed and answer. Her voice had sounded needy as if she needed someone to whom she could talk.

"What you want?" Toni managed to mutter, blocking the entrance to her room. She had no intentions of allowing Chocolate to enter her room. After all, she was the one who had made it very clear that she did not want to be in Toni's room anymore.

"To talk. I miss havin' somebody to talk to. We were friends before we were lovers. You are the one who taught me that it was possible for me to have female friends. Before you, I didn't get along with the opposite sex. I was always competin' with women. I was in the mind of thinkin' that a woman wasn't nothin' but a bitch who was out to get my money. Toni, don't make me explain all this again. You know me. You are the only person in the world who does know me.

"You came along and showed me different. Before tryin' to get at me, you were nice to me. Even when I turned my nose at you, you stuck it out. Even when I stated that we wouldn't be lovers, you waited for me and made me laugh. You made life a whole lot easier for me. I wish we had remained simply friends, 'cause I hated breakin' your heart. You was the only friend I have ever had. I guess that's what made you my best friend."

"Come on in and have a seat," Toni said, as she slowly opened the door. "Don't sit on my bed, though."

Chocolate sighed and entered the room. "I don't like how things is between us. How long is you gonna be mad at me? I miss havin' you as a friend. Your friendship was real important to me."

"Then why did you end it?"

"I didn't mean to end our friendship. I only wanted to end us makin' love to each other. Toni, I want things in life —things you cain't give. I want children. I want a husband. I want to stand in a packed church house and exchange vows with the man I intend to spend the rest of my life with. I didn't know it until recently. Once I realized what I wanted, I figured it didn't make sense to keep pretendin' with you. I didn't think it was fair. Just think about it. What if I was still pretendin' with you and some man came along and I up and left you? I didn't want to hurt you in that manner. I was simply tryin' to be honest, not hurtful."

"What you tried to do and what you ended up doing was 'bout the same in my eyes," Toni looked away as she spoke. She was afraid of her emotions. One minute she wanted to grab Chocolate and kiss her, the next minute she wanted to grab her and choke the life out of her. Looking away was the only action she could take to calm these mixed feelings.

"I didn't mean for it to be this way," Chocolate got up from the chair and sat on the bed next to Toni. "You the only person I ever gave a damn about in the entire world. That's a lot of carin', 'cause this is a big-ass world. Anybody else, I would have used up until they walked away from me. Toni, I have hurt some people in my lifetime. I have hurt some folks and didn't think two shits 'bout it. But you was different. You became my friend before you became my lover."

Chocolate gently took Toni's hands in hers then continued.

"Toni, you *are* my friend. It simply don't make sense for us to be living in the same place and acting like we is strangers. I know more 'bout you than anybody in this house. I know what makes you feel good. I know what makes you feel bad. I used to know how to stop you from hurting— that is, until I became the reason for your pain.

"You cain't blame me for wanting what Annie Mae has. I feels 'bout that child the same way you feels. I see the way you look at him when you hold him. He ain't somethin' you can create yourself. God made it so all us— even whores— can have babies. We let Madam Honey and all this money that hasn't added up to shit, trick us into believin' that we had it all.

"All the money in the world couldn't bring us the happiness that baby has brought us, and his happiness is borrowed. He can never belong to any of us. It seems to me that nothin' has stopped us from procreatin' but us.

"I'm not pointin' fingers 'cause I'm guilty of drinkin' her poison mixture to get rid of more than my share of babies. Delroy reminds me of my mistakes every time he smiles. I have to ask myself would one of my babies have had a smile as bright and gorgeous as his? Sad part is, I'll never know."

Without warning, Chocolate reached up and took Toni's handkerchief off her head saying, "Let me do something to your hair."

Toni got up from her bed, sat in the chair and, as she handed Chocolate a comb, said, "Delroy does make me want to have a baby. He reminds me of perfection. I only wonder if I can create somethin' to his likeness. Problem is, I don't know how to love men."

"You love them the same as you loved me. You talk like a man isn't normal. Truth be told, and no hard feelings Toni, but a man's love is more than a woman's. A man will give you more than a woman can ever give you, physically and mentally. A man you love will take you around the world simply by smilin' at you."

"I ain't never witnessed no man around these parts make a woman feel like you talkin'," Toni quipped.

"Men who enter this house aren't lookin' to make a woman feel good," Chocolate said laughing. "These men are lookin' to pay for their own pleasure — damn the woman who happens to be layin' under him when he's doin' the searchin'. Just 'cause these men enter this house don't mean they ain't good men. The same men who come here are the same men who love somebody a few miles down the road. They have families they would lay they lives down for. Us whores are simply somethin' for them to do. We are a way for them to relieve their frustrations."

"I like my hair," Toni said, changing the subject. "It looks good on me."

"We friends?" Chocolate asked, walking toward the door.

"Yes," Toni managed to say. "I'm glad you explained everything to me, 'cause I was thinkin' it was somethin' I did."

"I'm leavin'." Chocolate said, reaching for the doorknob. "I haven't told anyone, but I made up my mind and I'm goin'. I was hopin' I could mend things with you before I left."

"Why? Why you goin'?" Toni asked sadly alarmed.

"I been wantin' to go, but I never thought I had a reason. I would pack my bags and turn back around. Hell, I'd pack my bags and never step foot outside of my room. I was into thinkin' that life outside of this place wasn't gonna do me any good. I reasoned that my money was all I needed. I wasn't scared of outside. I just didn't think outside mattered.

"The other day I was watchin' Delroy and his momma. Watching that girl and her child, I then realized I was witnessing life and love for the first time. I realized that all my money and all my fine clothes didn't amount to shit. My inner knowledge enlightened me that that ratty girl and her fatherless child were worth more than my lifetime of nothin'. It's been in me all the time, wantin' to go. That's why I been savin'. I had me a nice stash until Delroy came along. I've spent a lot of money on him. I'm not mad at myself. I feel he's the only thing worth somethin' that I've spent money on. Delroy gave me the courage I needed to go. He gave me strength and reason. But before I left, I needed to know I had a friend."

"You have one," Toni said as Chocolate exited her room.

34

Annie Mae (The Silent Girl)

Annie Mae observed things going on around her and could tell the order of the house was falling apart. Pretty had taken off and, now, Chocolate was gone.

She had left and had not told anyone she was leaving. Madam Honey was *very* angry. As Annie Mae sat back and watched, it was obvious in the way the big woman yelled and lashed out at the few women left in the house that she was losing control.

She had even witnessed what had happened the day Lacey had walked off, never to return. Madam Honey had walked up to Lacey and told him in a rather rude way, "You goin' to have to help Toni clear the field. I cain't afford to pay Marcus any longer."

Without Marcus working, it meant she expected Lacey to take his place and do the job. Lacey informed Madam Honey, "I don't intend to clear nobody's field. And furthermore, I won't put myself in a situation where you pull your gun on me. I don't intend for you to kill me and get away with it." Lacey continued his speech and informed Madam Honey, "I won't disrespect you in any way. I promise I will leave your home."

The next thing Annie Mae knew, Lacey had headed for the front door—a door he never before had used.

Annie Mae observed Madam Honey's anger swell. She noticed it was the Sheriff who was able to work her up the most. She would beg and plead with him to give her more time to pay up, always reminding him of how good and honest she had been to him in the past. If he would only work with her, she would get her place back in order.

The Sheriff did not seem to care about Madam Honey's begging and pleading. He only pointed out the fact that she had lost hold of her girls when she allowed Annie Mae and her child in her home. To his way of thinking, they were the reason for all the bad luck Madam Honey had come across.

"I don't understand why a house full of whores is so smitten by a wayward woman and her bastard child..."

Obviously, the Sheriff hated the baby and his mother, Annie Mae. It was his hate that dictated Annie Mae's decision to stay at Madam Honey's a little longer.

Annie Mae spent most of her time in a corner of the house and laughed inside as Madam Honey's powerful image shrunk like an intimidated young girl whenever the Sheriff harassed and embarrassed her by calling her half-witted, obese, and soon-to-be-broke and jailed if she did not change things in her house. He called her what Annie Mae's husband had called her and worse. All the time the Sheriff harangued her, Madam Honey would keep her head down and plead for more time. She never even looked the Sheriff in the eyes when he yelled at her.

Secretly, Annie Mae enjoyed witnessing Madam Honey's power being taken away by the very white man who had given her the power to kill her husband.

After the Sheriff exited the house, things would get real rough for the whores who were still living there. It seemed Madam Honey was constantly yelling at them starting with the first one she saw.

The other day it had been Cherry. Madam Honey complained saying, "You ain't workin' hard enough! Stop drinkin' so much, too!"

Cherry muttered something under her breath about not taking a drink in months. Madam Honey must have thought she had sassed her because before one could blink, Madam Honey had slapped Cherry so hard it sent her across the room. Enraged, she had marched toward her to continue the beating. But, just then, Richard's crying and crawling towards Cherry stopped her from stomping the poor white girl into the floor. Richard was the only something that gave Madam Honey any peace of mind. He also was the very thing the Sheriff wanted gone from her house.

Just like that, Madam Honey's whole demeanor changed. She picked up Richard and started kissing and pleading with him not to cry. Annie Mae could see the love Madam Honey had for her child. She loved Richard and anything that had to do with him. Because she loved the boy, it meant she had to treat Annie Mae with respect. Madam Honey even agreed to start calling the boy Richard instead of Delroy. Of course, Annie Mae had to threaten to leave before she agreed.

35

Mary Ann Tobert (Bit-of-Honey)

Mary sat tucked away behind a tree reading the letter Pretty had sent her. She was glad she was the one who happened to receive the mail because, if Madam Honey had seen the letter first, Mary was not sure she would have gotten it. Ever since Chocolate had left, Madam Honey had not been in a good mood.

The income Chocolate had generated for Madam Honey had been considerable and, when she left, it greatly affected both Madam Honey's income and her relationship with Sheriff Jenkins. He had warned her that he did not know how long he could keep the law away from her place if she did not start paying the right amount.

Madam Honey had pleaded with him to give her more time. She reminded him she always made good on paying him back what she owed. Also, she told him that, any day, now a girl was bound to walk through the forest and up her steps. When the girl did, she promised she would be able to pay him. A few more days were all she needed in order to clear her debt. Sheriff Jenkins had just stormed off.

The truth of the matter was, Mary knew that business had slowed down considerably. All the colored johns were boycotting Madam Honey's place. It was the death of the last boy that had changed their minds. Mary had noticed the decrease in colored men visiting Madam Honey's. They had visited for a short while after the boy's death—two months to be exact. A few regulars had even come a week or two after the others had stopped coming. It was a fact that the white men spent more money, but it was the colored men who visited more often. The nickels and dimes of the colored men had added up and made the difference in Madam Honey's pocketbook.

Then, the colored regulars quit coming all together.

It was Cherry who informed Mary.

"When I visited town, I overheard a group of colored men talkin'. They specifically stated that they were upset about the death of the last young boy Madam Honey had killed. Thomas Lee had led the conversation. You know him. He used to be one of my regular johns. They decided that if Madam Honey was goin' to treat colored men the way white folks was treatin' them, then they would take their money elsewhere. So, instead of going to Madam Honey's, they have taken to goin' to women's homes."

Cherry also informed Mary, "I can always tell which woman has been sellin' pussy. It's by the new clothes they wearin' or the sacks they carryin' that are filled to the top with groceries. They don't have the usual half-empty bag, with beans and rice. These women are carryin' sacks that overflow with meat — good cuts, too. I only saw a few women in town walkin' about like that; walkin' around town with a look that let everybody know life was goin' to be a little easier for them and their children."

Mary shook the thought of what Cherry had told her out of her head and opened the letter and read to herself.

My Dear Friend Mary,

I hope this letter reaches your hands. First off, I want to thank you for giving me the insight to leave that wicked place. I walked away from that house not knowing what I was gonna do with myself. The only thing I knew was that I was gonna find different. I left feeling that, if I never had a man touch me again, I would die happy.

I walked until I reached the next town over, Spillman. I spent my week away from home sleeping in the streets. I had a few men offer me a place to stay for the night, but I turned them all down. Lying on the cold hard ground, I didn't even consider taking any of them up on their offer. I was determined to find me a place in this world that didn't include me trading myself for sex. The craziest thing about the whole situation was that I never worried the whole time I was homeless. I still carried myself in a way which led people to think I was important. I refused to lose my spirit because I was without shelter. I knew in my heart that leaving Madam Honey's was the best thing for me.

Anyways, the seventh day of my wandering, I came across a woman. The woman's name happened to be the same as yours, Mary. Mrs. Mary is a spunky sixty-five year-old lady. She's well off and real friendly. Mrs. Mary Coleman is her full name. Mrs. Mary is something else. She sat next to me one morning as I ate my breakfast in a rundown diner and engaged me in conversation. First, she wanted to know where I came from. Not wanting to be bothered, I told her I came from a whorehouse. She busted out laughing and told me she was sure glad I gathered my senses and left. From that moment on we were inseparable. When she found out I was homeless, she had me come stay with her. I told her I would only stay there if I could do some cleaning and that I was only gonna stay until I found me a real job and got my own place. You gotta laugh at the thought of me cleaning the shit off of toilets and grateful that God blessed me with a decent place to stay.

Mrs. Mary has a nice home. Her home makes Madam Honey's place look like a shack. She was married to some white man in England. She said the man invested in some stocks —that's how he made his fortune. Anyways, when he died, she moved back to the States. She said she was tired of living around uppity people and wanted to be around her own kind. Once she returned home, it wasn't what she thought it would be. She soon found out her people only wanted to deal with her for money. She informed me that she's been dealing with fake people so long she was in need of a person who wasn't smelling her farts and pretending they were perfume. You should see how folks run in behind her, putting on airs and hoping they can get something out of it —kind of like we used to do for johns. Anyways, it was at Mrs. Mary's house where I found the man of my dreams. His name is Carter.

Carter is Mrs. Mary's second cousin. Girl, Carter is a fine man. He's about six-two with smooth caramel skin, and a build that would have put him on the auction block for at least seven to ten thousand dollars. Chile, I tell you Carter is a man. His deep, brown bedroom eyes can take any woman's breath away. The sight of him made me want to pay him to sleep with me.

Carter simply popped in my life. Like I stated earlier, I wasn't looking for no man. All I was searching for was peace. I was into thinking that looking after Mrs. Mary was all the happiness I was entitled to, and I was fine with that. Carter is one of the few kinfolk that Mrs. Mary allows in her home. He isn't like the rest of her family. Mrs. Mary keeps most her family members away.

Carter took a liking to me the moment he laid eyes on me. I knew he was smitten, but I ignored him. I was in the mind of thinking he only wanted to sleep with me. Plus, there was the matter of Mrs. Mary to deal with. I knew she liked me. But I had told her about my past and I didn't know what she would think of me and her cousin becoming an item. To my surprise, it was her who insisted that I take Carter up on his offer and go out with him. From that point, my life with Carter has been like a fairytale. Mrs. Mary paid for the wedding and, as a wedding gift, she gave us a nice home in a really nice neighborhood. It all happened so fast! I haven't been gone a full year and I'm living a life I didn't dare think I would ever be a part of. My only regret is I didn't leave Madam Honey's sooner.

Pray that I have a baby, Mary. A child is all I want to make my life complete. It doesn't matter if I have a girl or a boy. My only wish is that a healthy baby one day grows in my womb. It's not too late for you, Mary. You don't have to stay in that wicked woman's house living under her rules. Don't do as I did and spend a lifetime making her rich. Leave! Leave as soon as you get this letter. I know you think that Travis fella was your only true love, but it's not so. There is a Carter out there for you, somewhere. I didn't know where my love was. God sent him to me. Things for you will never change if you stay in that house. Please keep my address and write me back. Better yet, come stay with me. You can live here until you decide what to do with yourself.
Your True Friend,
Saless Coleman

With a bemused smile on her face, Mary folded the letter as small as she could and stuck it inside her bra.

36

Toni (Rainie Holloway)

W hat you doin' out here?" Toni asked Marcus as he picked up the shovel and started working. In order to have a reason to leave the house, she had gotten up extra early. She had made two thick ham sandwiches, a jug of water, and had headed toward the field. Toni continued, "Madam Honey ain't gonna pay you nothin'. She ain't got no money for all that. She's just about broke. She ain't paid me in months. I don't bother her about it, though. She got enough problems tryin' to pay your evil cousin, Sheriff Jenkins."

"You think she'll feed me and send my aunt a plate if I keep workin'?" he asked hopefully.

"I don't know. You'll have to talk to her yourself," Toni went to her bag and handed Marcus one of her sandwiches before she went back to working. "I try to stay away from her nowadays," she continued. "The only thing that seems to settle her down is that baby boy."

"Is Madam Honey the one who gave Cherry a black eye?" Marcus asked conversationally as he ate the ham sandwich in two bites. It amazed Toni that he could open his mouth that wide. Toni made the meat extra thick because she wanted to make sure she had enough food to hold her until late in the day. She had no intentions of returning to the house until she had to.

Marcus continued to speak with his mouth full. When a piece of ham fell out of his mouth, he hurried and picked it up off the ground and ate it. Toni could only blink her eyes in shock as he ate the soiled piece of meat. He said, "I seen Cherry the other day in town drinkin'. I was too scared to ask her what happened. She looked real sad. If I'm not mistaken, I saw tears in her eyes. Like I said, I was scared to go near her, so I walked off. It wasn't that I didn't care. I just didn't know what to say to her. I never seen her in a condition like that. I'm used to seein' her smilin' and such."

"I figured that's where she headed off to when she left," Toni said, pausing from shoveling dirt. "For awhile there she had stopped drinkin'. It was Madam Honey slappin' her that started her back."

"Why she slap her?" Marcus asked.

"I don't know. I guess she frustrated by the way things around here is goin'. With Pretty and Chocolate gone, ain't much money comin' in. Not only that, the men don't come like they used to. Your cousin ain't lettin' up on her one bit. He wants her to put the boy and his momma out. He wants that bad." Toni walked over to a tree stump and took a break and Marcus silently followed. "Seems to me Madam Honey is willin' to lose it all over that boy."

"Why you think that?" Marcus was eyeing Toni's other sandwich. She knew he was hungry, so she gave it to him.

"I'm not sure. The one thing that I am sure of is that things is changin' around here for the worse."

"Like how?" Marcus asked, eying Toni's water.

She handed it to him before she continued. "Can you keep a secret? I haven't told anybody else what I'm 'bout to tell you. I used to go and talk to Madam Honey when I needed to talk, but nowadays, she's too mean to listen to anything I have to say.

"Spendin' all this time workin' with you, I learned you are good people, Marcus. We get along fine. You tell me things and I listen. I tell you things and you listen. One thing I've come to know is that nothin' I have told you has gotten back to anyone I've talked about."

Marcus stopped drinking the water when he realized Toni was indicating he was her friend. He had never had a friend before. During his whole life, children had made fun of him and stayed away. He was the only person in his school who was considered "special." That meant he had spent his lifetime being pointed and laughed at.

"I won't tell nothin' you tell me," he assured her.

"Lacey has sent word that he wants me to come and go with him. Cherry visited him and told him that Madam Honey was losin' her mind. She said Lacey wasn't worried 'bout nobody but me. He said he knew the rest of the girls could get along fine without Madam Honey, but he wasn't so sure about me."

"What you gonna do?" Marcus asked.

"I don't know. I know I cain't stay here too much longer. Sheriff Jenkins is bound to have the place raided sooner or later. I know if I go to jail, I'm gonna be stuck there. I don't have nobody to come bail me out."

"Maybe a new girl will come along before all that happens."

"Ain't no new girl comin' 'round here. Even if one does come, Madam Honey will run her off before she gets settled in. Truly, the woman *is* losing her mind."

"I hope something changes, 'cause I sure will miss you if you leave. I like being out here with you. I know I used to talk bad about you all before I really got to know you."

Marcus handed Toni her water and she took a deep gulp.

"This is the only place in town where people listen to me.

Everywhere else, I'm yelled at or made fun of."

"Actually, I don't want to leave but I feel as if Madam Honey is forcin' me go. After watching her hit Cherry like that, I know she's bound to shoot anyone of us. If it hadn't been for the baby, she was gonna give Cherry a real good beatin'. I just know it. What I don't know is why Lacey is lookin' after my wellbeing. I didn't know he cared for me. I thought he was Pretty's friend."

"You all are a family."

Seeing the startled look on Toni's face, Marcus felt he had to explain his statement.

"Least that's how I see it; that is, before Madam Honey started losin' her mind. What I saw was everybody takin' care of each other. You doin' the cookin', and all the other girls providin' the money to run the house. Larry was like the big brother that wears dresses. Didn't he step up to the plate when the baby girl died? He even wore a man's suit to the funeral. Seems to me," Marcus took another gulp of the water before continuing, "he don't want nothin' to happen to his little sister. You is the baby of the bunch. I can see why he's lookin' after you. It makes sense 'cause he was with Madam Honey for years."

"I never thought of it that way."

"You think she gonna let me work for some food? I sho' miss all that good cookin'."

"Ain't been much cookin' lately. We don't have nearly as many men come visit anymore. Madam Honey usually has me put the leftovers up for the next day. She might let you work 'cause ain't nobody else willin' to do it."

"I sure hope so," Marcus said, thinking about all the leftovers he would be able to consume.

"Your aunt gonna let you work without receivin' money for your services? I know she liked all the food Madam Honey was sendin', but I'm sure she would prefer money."

Marcus gave a little smile and replied, "What she wants and what I'm gonna do is two different things. I figure as long as I keep up with goin' to church, she won't care what I'm doin'. If she ask me 'bout it, I'll lie. Maybe I'll talk the Sheriff into askin' her if I can work for somethin' to eat. He knows firsthand that my aunt doesn't have enough money to feed me properly. He also knows Madam Honey cain't afford to pay me. Plus, I figure if I take half of what you all give me home, my aunt will be satisfied. She may complain and make like she needs me to work for money. The truth is, she speaks details concernin' how she misses the good meals Madam Honey used to send me home with. I overheard her braggin' 'bout the up-side-down peach cake you sent me home with one time. She was tellin' the preacher's wife she never tasted somethin' so good in all her days. Said she could taste the sweet peaches in her mouth a week after she ate it. So, I'm more than sure my aunt will accept the food."

"Well," Toni said finishing off what little water was in the bottle, "it's gonna have to be you that asks Madam Honey 'bout workin', 'cause, like I said earlier, I try to stay clear of her."

Changing the subject Marcus suddenly asked, "When you fix your hair up? I ain't never seen you without your hat on. You look like a girl— a pretty girl at that."

Toni blushed before she answered. "Chocolate showed me how to do it before she left. It looked better earlier, before I started sweatin'. I cain't put it up the way she did, but I'm gettin' better at it."

"It still looks pretty. Toni, if I ask you somethin', you promise not to get mad at me? The last thing I want to do is make you mad at me. Not even ten minutes ago, you told me we was friends. If me askin' you somethin' will mess that up, I'd soon as keep it to myself."

"You can ask me whatever you please," Toni stopped shoveling and looked Marcus in the face. The expression on his face said he was scared of what he was about to say. "I promise I won't be mad at you, Marcus. I know whatever it is you ask me is only 'cause you want to know somethin' 'bout me. I'm your friend, Marcus. Go ahead and speak."

"Well..." he gulped then continued, "I know you and Chocolate was datin' and all. I also know ya'll broke it off. You never looked like this when you was goin' out with her. You always looked like a man. Now that you look different, is you gonna start datin' men?"

"I'm...I'm gonna try," Toni said the words so low, she barely heard herself speak them. "I'm gonna try. I'm gonna take Chocolate's advice and love the way God intended me to love."

"I hope it works out for you. Regardless of what you decide to do, I'm gonna be your friend. I like you, Toni. I like you a whole lot."

As he spoke, Marcus turned and spotted Madam Honey on the porch. "I'm gonna go and talk to her now. I hope she lets me help you out."

37
Mary Ann Tobert (Bit-of-Honey)

When Mary stepped into her room, Annie Mae was sitting on her bed. This startled her. The time was around two in the morning and her room was pitch black. Though the last customer had left, Mary was not tired. Her body was still accustomed to working until sunrise— when Madam Honey had had a house packed with men, that is. Those days were long gone and the house was now starting to show the signs of being neglected. It seemed to Mary that the house was falling apart right under her feet. Now only one of the upstairs bathrooms worked properly and the front porch step was leaning. The roof was leaking in the kitchen and the yard looked a plum mess.

"I didn't know you were still up," Mary said to Annie Mae as she sat on the bed beside her.

"I been up for awhile. I guess all that sleepin' I done when I first arrived messed up my normal sleepin' pattern. I used to sleep like normal people—at night. Now I go days without sleepin'. Then, when I do finally fall asleep, I sleep for a long time. With the type of work you doin', it seems to me you should sleep a lot more than you do," Annie Mae observed.

"Chile, what you witnessin' ain't nothin'. Used to be, I'd have twenty or thirty men a night. Those few men you saw comin' in tonight wasn't nothin'."

Mary sat next to Annie Mae on the bed. "I think those days are long gone. Between you and me, Madam Honey is gonna have to find another way to bring some money in her home. I hope she saved up enough money to live on. Sheriff Jenkins ain't gonna permit her to keep runnin' this business if she don't figure out a way to come up with the money to pay him. I was thinkin' 'bout tellin' her to open up some type of eatin' establishment. Folks love her cookin'."

"Why don't you mention it her?" Anne Mae said as she shifted her body away from Mary. The foul smell the men had left on Mary's body turned her stomach.

"Scared."

"Why you scared?"Annie Mae asked, moving closer to the edge of the bed.

"Madam Honey is goin' crazy. She stays mad all the time. I'm afraid if I say anything to her 'bout the way she runnin' her business, she'll get mad at me. You saw how she attacked Cherry for no reason at all."

Anne Mae gave her thoughts saying, "The woman has always seemed a bit off to me. What type of older lady would sell young girls out? And she does it with a smile on her overblown face. I don't get how she makes like she gives a damn 'bout you all. I've seen folks treat animals better. The craziest part is the fact that you all do what you do with a smile on your faces. Before the men stopped comin', you all would walk around here happy as two faggots locked up in a one-man cell."

"Things was better," Mary mumbled.

"Things was better 'cause you all were keepin' her pocketbook fat. Now that it's a little lean, she showin' you all what you're worth. If you cain't see the truth, then maybe this is the way you need to spend your life."

"Why you talkin' down to me, Annie Mae? You forgot I'm the one who looked after you when you was down. It was me who cleaned your shit and kept the bed bugs from crawlin' all over your weak body."

"I ain't talkin' mean, Mary. I'm talkin' facts. I ain't forget nothin' you have done for me. You ever stop to think that perhaps your treatment of me is why I'm givin' you all this honesty?"

Mary sat in the dark room not knowing how to respond to Annie Mae's last remark. Then she replied, "She didn't force me to come. I came lookin' for her. She didn't even have to sanction me to stay. I know she seems like a mean woman to you. That's only 'cause you arrived while she in a bad situation."

"When I stepped on Madam Honey's porch, I didn't have nothin' but the clothes on my back. It was Madam Honey who gave me somethin' to put on." Mary hoped that her comments would clear some of the misconceptions Annie Mae was witnessing.

Shaking her head, Anne Mae said, "Madam Honey only gave you the clothes 'cause she had plans for you to take them off later. It wasn't no love involved in the reason for her givin' you somethin' to wear. "

"You don't understand, Annie Mae. I couldn't go back home. I couldn't face my momma being a failure."

"Oh, you think sellin' your body makes you a winner? Whatever it was you did to your momma cain't be worse than this."

"Well, this place cain't be that bad. You haven't left!" Mary snapped back. She could feel the anger rise as she spoke the words.

"I ain't doin' what you doin' either, now am I? I'm gonna leave," Annie Mae stood as she spoke. "I'm gonna leave sooner than you think. Right now, I'm simply doin' to Madam Honey what she been doin' to all you. I'm usin' her. I'm not leavin' until I see her broke down— broke down the way I was when I walked on her property. It took me a long, hard journey to get here. Now that I'm here, I'm gonna follow through with my plans."

"I ain't a bad person." Mary said, deciding to change the subject. She did not know how to respond to Annie Mae's last statement. She knew Annie Mae was upset with Madam Honey, but she was not sure why. Mary also knew that if she wanted to tell the reason for staying until she broke Madam Honey down, she would have told her.

"You like layin' up with men for money?" Annie Mae asked, looking directly in Mary's face. The room was dark, but Mary could tell by the closeness of Annie Mae that she was looking in her direction.

"It's a job. I used to like the pay, but it ain't like it used to be."

"If the money ain't right, then why you doin' it? Why you still here? You plan on doin' this the rest of your life? What you gonna do when you get old?" Anne Mae asked.

"Nobody plans on doin' this for the rest of they life." The attitude in Mary's voice was thick.

"You need to start plannin' your next move." Annie Mae said and walked out of Mary's room.

38

Cherry (Heather Lee Witman)

Why you love me, Marcus Huckenberry? You been snoopin' 'round me forever looking all wide-eyed and silly, proclaimin' I'm what you want as a wife. All along as I can remember, you been actin' a fool behind me. You don't even know what I feel like in bed. I ain't never understood that. For once, can you please tell me why you think I'm so special? My own momma didn't think I was shit!"

Marcus sat on Madam Honey's porch across from Cherry. He remained silent as he did not know how to respond. In fact, he could not even look her in the face when she spoke.

"Just as I thought. You full of shit like other men who done looked me in the eyes and told me how beautiful I am. You hear me talkin' to you, Marcus? I know you ain't retarded. Your arm just bad. I want to know why it is you claim to love me and don't tell me it's 'cause I'm pretty. I done heard that so much it turns my damn stomach."

Cherry rolled her eyes and picked up a small pebble and hit Marcus on the leg.

"I'd be lying if I didn't say it had something to do with how you look," Marcus managed to say.

"I don't wanna hear nothin' 'bout my looks. My looks is why I was left here to sell my body."

Marcus looked up and saw the permanent mark that was now a part of Cherry's face thanks to Madam Honey. It was a small piece of thick skin under her right eye.

Most people would not have noticed it, but Marcus knew what Cherry had looked like before the beating Madam Honey put on her.

"I've always thought you were a special person. Your looks have a lot to do with my thinkin'. But it's your strength that stands out most."

"You is crazy," Cherry said with a hint of anger in her voice.

"Now, don't you go callin' me names, Cherry. I don't think that's fair. You the one who asked me a question. I'm only answerin' what you asked."

"Well, you need to explain to me why you think I'm strong. If I was so strong, don't you think I would have enough sense to fight back when Madam Honey attacked me for nothin'?"

"No. Then I would have thought you was crazy. We both know she would have killed you —killed you and nothin' would have happened. Folks in town would have been talkin' 'bout a mad whore who needed to be put in the ground.

"I think you did what was best. I think you a strong person 'cause you found a way to make it without your momma. Take me, for instance; I have to depend on my aunt."

"You don't have to. You could leave."

"And go where? Folks take one look at me and swear on a stack of Bibles that I ain't got it all. Folks had me thinkin' I didn't have it all. It wasn't till I started working here that I was able to say somethin' without being laughed at. Even before I started workin', you would talk to me. Madam Honey would run me off, but not you. You would sit on the porch and treat me like a human being. I liked that type of treatment. I like you for bein' nice to me. I'm gonna be honest. I fell in love with you when I first laid eyes on you.

"Before we spoke, I thought you was gonna be weak. I thought because yo' momma ran off and left you, you was gonna be walkin' 'round feelin' sorry for yourself. I used to. I used to find me a quiet place and cry. I had to go somewhere I could cry without being yelled at for wasting tears. My aunt Dorothy will yell at me for just about anything. It wasn't till I got to know you that I figured I didn't have no right to be cryin'. Hell, if anybody should be cryin', it should be you.

"Every time I saw you, you was full of smiles. All except that time I spoke on your momma. I left thinking you was gonna stay mad at me, but you didn't. You forgave me in no time. The next time I came 'round, you treated me like I had never said anything mean about her."

Cherry was not prepared for the response Marcus gave her. She could tell the words he spoke were the truth. The look in his eyes was an honest look.

"I ain't never had a man speak such nice words to me and be tellin' the truth," she whispered.

"I ain't lyin', Cherry. I'm tellin' you what you deserve to hear."

"I know," Cherry said with tears in her eyes. "All this time people been thinkin' you were a retard. If only folks was to sit down and talk to you, they would find out how much of a smart man you are."

"I ain't gonna sit here and allow you to call me smart. Still, I won't accept dumb, anymore."

"Marcus, if you see me as being strong, I think I have the right to see you as being smart." Cherry stood up, walked over and lightly kissed him on his head.

39
Madam Honey (Abigail Richard)

Bring me that boy!" Madam Honey instructed Cherry as she sat in the kitchen eating leftover chicken backs and mashed potatoes from the night before. She placed Richard on the table and started spooning him the potatoes. Richard had gotten quite big. Madam Honey had introduced him to solid food a month after he was born. She was quick to spoon flavorful bean juice in his mouth. She was also known to chew chicken and greens up, then take the food out of her mouth and feed it to the baby. Richard laughed after each bite and kicked his legs in the air.

"Madam Honey's baby boy is gettin' bigger every day," she smiled and cooed to him using baby talk. "I know you done grown at least an inch since I laid eyes on you yesterday. You is Madam Honey's pride and joy. I love me some Richard. I know you loves me, too."

Madam Honey fed the baby until he refused to eat anymore.

"How long Lacey been stayin' at Martha's house?" she asked Cherry, without taking her eyes off of Richard.

"Since he walked away from here."

"Sheriff Jenkins said he done seen him in town a couple of times since walkin' out. What plans he got?" She looked Cherry straight in the eyes as she spoke. The tone of voice she used let Cherry know she meant business.

"He don't go into details about his plans. The only thing he mentions is that he's gonna leave from here."

Cherry knew better than to reveal that Lacey was planning on moving to Harlem and taking Toni with him.

He had informed Cherry, "In Harlem we can be the type of people we want to be. I've grown tired of wearing pants and dressing like a man. Inside of Madam Honey's house, I dressed as I'm pleased. Since walking out the door, I had to wear the same outfit I bought for the baby's funeral. It was that same outfit I wore to Martha's until she made me a few pair of jeans and men's shirts."

Lacey also told Cherry, "At first I was scared to venture into town. I was afraid I would be attacked. Men who like men are usually not treated well in small towns. After a couple of days of staying in Martha's house, I finally took a chance and went into the colored bar. That's where I met you and I told you of my plans to leave."

Lacey had mentioned to Cherry, "I have saved well over five thousand dollars. I intend to take my money and Toni, and relocate to a place where I don't have to wait until the sun sets to go outside."

Madam Honey's voice broke into her thoughts by saying, "Sheriff Jenkins said he's seen the both of you talkin'. He said you been spendin' plenty of Sundays with him. I know he tellin' you somethin' about his plans."

"Madam Honey, he ain't talkin' 'bout no plans," Cherry lied, shaking her head. "Mostly, he talkin' about how messed up and closed-minded this town is. It's hard for him bein' the way he is outside your house. He don't like it. He don't like nothin' 'bout livin' among people who don't understand his way of livin'."

"Well, I didn't make him leave. He left on his own accord. He's welcome to come back. Tell him if he comes back, I won't be askin' him to work outside. I need his earnin's. That damn Marcus is 'bout to eat me out of house and home."

"I'll let him know next Sunday," Cherry promised.

Madam Honey sat quietly for a moment. "You think maybe it would be better if I went and spoke to him myself?"

Cherry could not believe what she was hearing. Madam Honey never left the house. In fact, she could not recall Madam Honey ever stepping off the porch since her momma had dropped her off there.

"You think maybe you could tell him to come to me?" The look on Cherry's face must have informed her that she was looking desperate. The last thing Madam Honey wanted was to be portrayed as weak.

"Yea, that would probably be best. I'll have him come here next time I meet up with him." Cherry stood up to leave the kitchen, but not before taking the baby and giving him to his momma.

Madam Honey rocked back and forth in her chair at the kitchen table. When she noticed she was rocking, she stopped herself. To her, rocking was a sign of having bad nerves and she had not exhibited that emotion in years. It had only been since Sheriff Jenkins had been coming around protesting about the girls not making enough money that her nerves were on edge.

Lost in her thoughts she asked herself: *'Why cain't I get customers to come anymore? It just don't make sense. For years things been runnin' smooth. I used to keep a house full of horny men. They would be standin' in the hallways waitin' their turn to have a good time. Here, lately, my place been empty. A few white men have trickled in and out of the house, but not enough to keep the Sheriff happy and certainly not enough to keep money in my pocket. I know the only thing holding the Sheriff off is the fact that I been payin' him from my private stash. Used to have a pretty penny saved, twenty thousand dollars to be exact and I was lookin' forward to the day I could retire. I had envisioned my last days with no money problems whatsoever. Now, the men not comin' to my place is changin' that fast. With no backup plan, I don't know how to handle the lack of cash flow. Today, my savings are almost dried up. My only hope is that the men will soon return. I need them in order to make my establishment what it used to be.*

'If only I could get a new girl— a real pretty one; a girl who looked as good as Pretty would put me back in the game in no time. Pretty was the only woman I ever saw who could drive men to spendin' plenty of cash without goin' about the house half-naked, but simply on pure beauty.

'Maybe if word got out that I had a new girl, perhaps the men would return. Used to be when one girl left, another one took her place. That's what happened the day Mary walked up my steps. Violet wasn't long gone before Mary showed up needin' work.'

It seemed no new girls were in town. In the past, Sheriff Jenkins had always notified Madam Honey whenever a new, young, pretty face popped up in town. But now he was always complaining about not getting his right pay. Madam Honey knew the town had to be full of the same drab homely looking women.

Whenever the Sheriff came, he put the blame for business being slow on the baby. For some reason, he thought that Richard had run the men off. In his mind, the men were tired of waiting for Mary to change diapers and tired of hearing a baby cry when they were trying to get a nice piece of tail.

Sheriff Jenkins hated the baby and he hated the baby's momma.

"You needs to get rid of her and her child! The damn girl look so homely you cain't even put her to work. You spendin' too much money on her and that illegitimate child."

Those words were always used in reference to Annie Mae and Richard. After he would leave, Madam Honey would try and talk herself into putting both of them out, but she could not bring herself to do it. She was in love with the boy; his mother was just there because of him. From the moment she had laid eyes on that baby, he had her. Madam Honey's heart had only been broken once since the child was born—the day his momma advised her to stop calling him Delroy and that he was to be named after his father, Richard. Madam Honey agreed because she knew she had no right to name another woman's child. Still, when no one was around, she called him Delroy.

40
Marcus Huckenberry

Marcus left the house knowing he would never be returning. He did not feel bad about leaving his aunt Dorothy alone because, all his life, he had been made to feel he was a burden to the woman. Not a day had passed that she did not remind him how she had taken him in because of his worldly mother. His aunt constantly reminded him that it was his mother's sins that had made him born with a defected hand; that it was his mother's drinking that had put her in an early grave. Had it not been for the love she had had for her sister, Marcus would have been left to fend on his own.

This was the veil of shame under which he had lived while growing up. When he was younger, he had been upset with his mother. Between his aunt and the bible, he had it in his mind that his momma was an evildoer. It was not until he got older, about thirteen, that he realized it was all right to love his mother. His reasoning was that she was his mother and if she was what God gave him then he was going to love her. He had long grown tired of hearing his mother being talked about as if she was not human.

Quietly, Marcus slipped out the back door of his aunt's house, but not before leaving four hundred dollar bills on the kitchen table.

He had never seen that much money in his life. Cherry had given the money to him and instructed him to leave it for his aunt.

He had tried desperately to talk her out of it because Marcus did not think she deserved it. In his argument, he reminded Cherry of all the immoral things his aunt had said about her. But she had just waved her hand in the air and told him to leave the money anyway.

Cherry's way of looking at the situation was that she figured his aunt would mourn when she found out Marcus had left. She felt the money would lessen problems for her. At least it would free her mind with regard to agonizing over how she was going to pay bills for awhile. With Marcus gone, she would not be able to hire him out. Cherry also informed him that once they were settled, they would try to send his aunt something every month. Even though Marcus did not agree with her, he did as he was told. He was thinking they would need the money for the life they intended to build together.

Marcus still could not believe what he had heard the day Cherry had walked up to him when he was working in the field. Of course, he had noticed her approaching him, but he did not get nervous about her presence anymore. He had it in his mind that he and Cherry were only going to be friends, which he thought was a good thing. Her being a friend was all right by him.

She had stood quietly beside him with tears in her eyes. It must have been a full five minutes before she spoke. "I know why she left. I'm not mad at her anymore. It was you who made me understand why I had no right to be mad at her anymore. She left 'cause she found somebody who loved her, in spite of what other people thought 'bout her. You got the same kind of love in you that that man had for my momma. I'd be a fool not to let you take care of me, Marcus."

"You serious, Cherry?" Marcus dropped his shovel and looked her in the eyes. "You mean it when you say you gonna allow me to love you? I been tryin' my whole life and now you stand here and tell me you really love me?"

"Yep. We gonna have to go to a place where we can love in peace— a place folks won't make fun of you 'cause of your hand, a place folks don't know my momma left me to be a child whore."

"Where you wanna go?" he asked excitedly with hope shining from his eyes.

"Harlem. That where Lacey and Toni gonna go. It's up north. I hear folks are real liberal up that way. It's in New York. Life is different for colored folks in Harlem. I figure if Lacey and Toni can live in peace, we can too. I don't wanna go nowhere where I have to pretend I'm all white. I wanna be me. I wanna be able to tell folks my momma was part black. I love my momma, no matter what she was. I know you, of all people, can understand that. I pretend too much with my johns. I simply wanna be real. You do love me enough to allow it, don't you?"

"Yes. I've always loved you," he assured her.

"Well, then you gotta love me with my clothes off." Cherry took Marcus by his nub and led him deep into the forest.

Four months had passed since they had shared their bodies with each other. At that time, Cherry had informed Marcus she had some money saved, but she needed a little more. Three thousand dollars was the total she had stashed away, but she insisted she needed to make a little more.

Now, today was the day they planned on leaving. Marcus was not sure how he was going to make a living in the city, but knew he was going to make it work. Cherry giving him the possibility to leave town and recreat himself was a gift from God. People in Harlem might see him and think of him as a retard, but once he opened his mouth, he refused be pushed aside. Once he opened his mouth and began speaking, they would know that his brain was just as sharp as theirs. The feeling of a new beginning excited him.

The first thing they planned to do when they entered Harlem was find a place of their own. Though he wanted to marry Cherry, he knew the law would not allow it. Even though they were going north, things had not changed to the point where they could legally be husband and wife. But Marcus reasoned that God could not blame him for the stupid laws of men. Also, he believed God knew how much he cared for Cherry. It was God who had brought the two orphaned lovers together, was it not?

Even though Marcus had never heard of Harlem before Cherry had mentioned it to him, he had told her he would go. All he knew was that he was willing to follow this woman to hell if she asked him to.

In his good hand, Marcus carried his suitcase walking with his head in the air, feeling proud of the new life he was about to embark upon. For the first time of his life, he was not afraid. The thought of his cousin, Sheriff Jenkins, seeing him walking with the suitcase did not bother him. In fact, he did not even try to come up with a lie just in case he was caught leaving. He felt he had no reason to lie.

When he boarded the bus through the front door and sat in the white section, Cherry, Toni, and Lacey boarded through the back door in the colored section. Marcus wanted badly to go and sit with his lover and friends, but he knew better. Even though he was changing, the world remained the same.

41

Mary Ann Tobert (Bit-of-Honey)

She broke her," Mary announced sitting across the table from Pretty, who was now five months pregnant. Mary was not used to seeing her friend with extra weight on her body. It made Mary smile to herself when she remembered how Pretty had been the only woman who had lived at Madam Honey's, who worried about her figure.

"That Annie Mae waited and then as soon as Cherry and Toni left, she packed her baby boy and walked out of the house. It wasn't long after she left that Sheriff Jenkins came through."

"Well, it sounds to me as if that girl was able to do what nobody else in that town could do—break both Madam Honey and Sheriff Jenkins."

"It was a sad sight watching Madam Honey sell all her belongings."

"It couldn't have been no sadder than watchin' Cherry bein' sold as a child. She was a baby when she came to that woman's house. Madam Honey should have seen her as a child. Instead, she saw the girl as profit. I cain't find it in my heart to feel sorry for the fat demon. I just cain't, Mary," insisted Pretty

"Maybe if you had seen it, you'd feel different," Mary said sadly.

"I don't think so," Pretty said, sipping on lemon water. "What I don't understand is why she had to leave the house. I was under the impression that she owned it."

"She did. But in order to keep the business goin', she had to sign the deed over to Sheriff Jenkins. Either that or he was goin' to have her arrested. I guess she thought business would pick up. When things never did, he came and had her put out of her own house," Mary explained.

"So, it wasn't hers, anymore," Pretty commented.

"Not only did he put her out, he had her hauled off to jail."

"That lowlife son-of-a-bitch! You mean to tell me he put Madam Honey in jail? After all the money she made for his white ass! I'll tell you the truth, Mary, he could have at least permitted her to have her freedom. It wasn't like she was plottin' against him. I'm pretty sure he knew the woman was tryin'. I guess her time was over. Nothin' lasts forever. She had paid him more than his share of money for nothin' long enough."

Pretty had thought she would be glad to hear of Madam Honey's suffering, but the Sheriff had taken things too far. No, none of this made sense.

"How did you manage to get away from the house without going to jail?" she asked Mary.

"I wasn't far from the house when they came to get her. I took off in the forest. Quickly, I ducked behind a tree and watched the whole thing. Boy was he mad! He yelled 'bout Marcus runnin' off with Cherry and the faggot. He even slapped Madam Honey to the ground. He accused her of knowin' Marcus and Cherry was leavin' together. Seems to me, the harder she tried to plead her case, the worse he beat her. In fact, he beat her so bad that it took four men to haul her into the bed of his truck. Personally, I think he planned it that way 'cause he never before drove his truck out to Madam Honey's."

"Well, I hate to hear all that, but I still say she brought it all on herself," Pretty said. "What goes around comes around. From the sound of things, Madam Honey is getting' hers tenfold."

42

Madam Honey (Abigail Richard)

Madam Honey sat on the floor of the dank, dark cell. Her eyes were swollen shut. Whenever she tried to open them, they were burned by the urine-filled air. She knew the urine she smelled was both hers and the others who had been housed in the small compartment. Though she was not sure, she thought her jaw might be broken. In fact, her entire face throbbed with pain and her body was not feeling much better.

The beating Sherriff Jenkins had given her at her house was bad enough, but it was the beating afterwards —when she had managed to grab a hold of Sheriff Jenkins and choke the life out of him— that hurt her the most. Though Madam Honey had felt the blows the men had landed on her body, the thrill of hurting Sheriff Jenkins had blocked out all the suffering her body was taking. It was only after she heard his last breath that she released his limp body and recognized all the agony her body had received.

While sitting on the floor of her small cell, Madam Honey figured she was going to die. In her mind, she reminded herself that at least she was going to die with a little piece of her dignity. For once in her life she had stood up to what had frightened her the most—men. She had grown tired of running from men. If she was not running from them, she was running to them. When she bought that piece of property way off in the woods, it was with the intention to be self-sufficient.

Then Sheriff Jenkins had come along, pushed himself on her and forced his way into her life and her pocketbook. With no other option, she had settled on his way. Yet, every time he stepped foot in the house she had paid for, it was his intent to disrespect her in front of her girls. Each time he arrived, she forced a smile on her face, transforming herself into a house slave by playing the role she had watched her grandmother play. Yet, she had been willing to do it as long as she got something out of the deal. The riches she received were a good enough reason for her to play the role of a happy house nigga.

It was Sheriff Jenkins forcing Annie Mae and her baby to leave that changed Madam Honey's spirit. When the baby left, she no longer bothered to smile or give excuses about owing him money. She simply looked him in the eye, with an *'I don't give a fuck'* expression. All the agonizing about his money was over.

Now, while sitting on the floor, Madam Honey suddenly realized she was heartbroken. She had not known it at the time because she had not allowed herself to develop feelings for anyone in so long that she had not recognized it until now exactly what she was feeling. At the time she had been so caught up in the fear of the child leaving that she had been confused. Though she complained out loud about not having any money coming in, on the inside she had been worrying about the child and his momma walking out.

When Sheriff Jenkins had arrived at her house with his men and the pickup truck, she had known the deal. Madam Honey knew he was going to cart her off to jail. She could accept jail. What she could not accept was not seeing Delroy, or Richard, as his momma called him, waking up smiling in her face.

While Sheriff Jenkins and his men had beat her, the tears that fell from her beady brown eyes were not for herself but for the new love of her life, the love that Sheriff Jenkins had forced to leave—Delroy.

On the ride to the jail she plotted how she could make him pay for what he had taken from her. Once they entered the jailhouse and he came over to taunt her, she immediately went into action. She somehow managed to reach up and squeeze the life out of his neck. Even with the men beating her, she continued to hold on.

Idly, Madam Honey wondered when her hanging would take place. She knew the people would turn out in droves to witness her demise, as she was not the most liked person in town. The hanging was going to happen—even if she had enough money to get herself a good lawyer. No one could get her off because a colored woman killed a white man— the Sheriff, at that. She knew she was going to have to pay for the sweet sensation of finally getting to take life from what she hated so much.

"You know you gonna die, nigga?" The anger in his voice was strong. Madam Honey turned her ear toward the sound. In vain, she tried to make out the voice of the person who was talking, but did not recognize it.

"They gonna hang yo' big black ass from a tree. It's gonna happen sooner than you think. We won't be wasting the county's money on no trial for you. Just know you gonna die soon."

Madam Honey closed her eyes and found the same comfort she had found when she first had laid eyes on little Delroy. Knowing she would never have to fear a man again gave her peace of mind. Never before had she been able to live without the fear of some man—white or black. Once in her life, she had tried loving a black man, but he up and left her for a white woman.

At this very moment, none of that mattered. For the first time in her life, the favorable sensation of liberation embraced her sore body.

'Everybody has to die,' she thought. Dying seemed like something she could do without any trouble stepping in the way.

'I'm gonna die,'

Out loud she said, "Well, it ain't a bad trade off. The world's gonna lose two evil people. Maybe things will be better for the living once I'm gone. Now that Sheriff Jenkins is out of the way, just maybe some poor colored girl can sell her ass and not have to pay a white man to let her do it."

www.ingramcontent.com/pod-product-compliance
Lightning Source LLC
Chambersburg PA
CBHW031403250626
47155CB00004B/1389